LOST AND FOUND

"SAVED BY GRACE"

Brittany K Moore

All characters within the pages of this book are fictitious. Any similarities between reality and those in the book are completely coincidental. All events within the pages of this book are fictitious. They are developed from the inner workings of the author's mind and should be taken as so.
Quotes have been taken from the NKJV of the Bible to be used in reference as well as guidance in this book. Copyright of the Bible is not the Authors right, but has been included as a reference point and should be taken as such.
First printing;
ISBN- 979-8-9861839-0-9
2 Get Moore Publishing- 2getmoorepublishing.com

Dedication:

To my readers who struggle, grasping for acceptance from the outside world. Broken hearted and dealing with mountains I cannot even fathom. Turn your heart to GOD, the one who can truly fill the emptiness in your soul and calm the raging storm.

Note to my readers:

This novella has depictions of loss, overcoming heartbreak, alcoholism, drug addiction, and quotes from the Bible. I meant all aspects of this story to encourage, uplift, and provide support.

This novella is a retelling of "The Woman at the Well" with depictions of Ruth, faith, strength, change, and above all LOVE from many other stories in the Bible.

John 4:39 (NKJV)

And many of the Samaritans of that city believed in him, because of the word of the woman who testified, "He told me all that I ever did."

"So often, the calling we receive from God is the one thing we couldn't see ourselves accomplishing."

-Brittany K Moore

Table of contents

CHAPTER ONE

Annoyance

My bottle of wine glared at me, or maybe I glared at it? The picture of glass shards as they exploded across my wooden coffee table where a welcome addition to my ever-changing imagination. I didn't know why, but I was so angry with that bottle and everything else going on in my life. My hand gripped a chicken nugget, and I ripped off a freezer burned mouthful, chewing the piece numbly as I continued to glare at the bottle.

Wrappers from the mini-Kit-Kat bars I had been munching on surrounded the bottle like a messed-up offering. My phone vibrated as I took another mouthful and I glared at that too, like it was the very thing tearing my life apart. Why was I so fed up with everything?

I grasped the bottle and rolled my eyes. Yeah, definitely not answering. Not mentally sound enough for that conversation. I tipped the bottle back and took a large swig. The glass clanked against my teeth before the liquid filled my mouth. Bitter, cheap, and worthless. Just like me.

My phone vibrated again. Ugh! My mom's name flashed across the screen. Didn't she realize I was wallowing in self-pity and wasn't in the mood to talk? I swirled the bottle around. The liquid sloshed a bit into my lap, and I giggled a manic giggle. My phone continued to vibrate. I glanced sidelong at it. It'd shimmied it's way across the table and was about to fall off. I sighed heavily before leaning forward right as it toppled over. Simultaneously, I slammed the bottle on the stupid coffee table.

"Hey Mom, kind of drinking my sorrows away. Can I call you tomorrow?"
"Nevaeh Serenity, don't be so dramatic. God has bigger plans for you than drowning yourself in a bottle of cheap alcohol. How's Naphtali?"

"First, his name is Nate, and he's out of the picture. Second, how do you know it's cheap? Third, alcohol is a good starting point till I figure out what this almighty God's plan is. Besides, Jesus drank wine."

"He drank it. He didn't swim in it. What do you mean Nate is out of the picture? He's your husband."

I huffed out a breath and rolled my eyes. They traveled to the bottle, and I chewed on my lip. It was always about faith in this, God that. Never just a; "Hey how's life, Nevey? Still falling apart? Man, I'm sorry, honey." Nope. Just; "God has a plan." Yeah, I'm calling total bull hockey. From what I understood, God hadn't been seen or heard of in over two thousand years. As far as I was concerned, he didn't exist anymore. If he ever did at all.

"Nevaeh?"

"Huh? Oh, Mom, I do not. I don't mean Nate literally is. But, really, if you think about it-"

"Don't you say it."

"You're the one who cursed me."

"I blessed you, young lady. They foretold it, you-"

"Yeah, yeah, I would be a beacon of hope. A testimony. What did you call for, Mom?"

I felt bad, but I wasn't in the mood for her Bible thumping right now.

"Well," her voice stuttered out.

I ran a hand through my hair, feeling suddenly like a stone had dropped into my stomach. "Spit it out, woman."

"I found some more of your father's things."

I pursed my lips. My father had passed away several months ago, and she was slowly making her way through all his stuff. She always told me she'd found more, even if it was a bucket of useless Knick Knacks.

I reached forward while shaking my head and grasped the bottle. I mustered up the energy to feign interest. “That’s great, Mom. What did you find this time?”

“Umm… well, that’s the thing. It’s a box addressed to you, and well… to God.”

I sat up straight. The bottle poised at my lips. “What?”

“It’s a box of letters… at least what I’m assuming are letters. I just opened it quickly, saw it addressed to you-”

“I heard you, but I don’t understand why.”

“Well, I… I don’t know. I never realized he was writing. You know how secretive your father could be sometimes.”

“Yeah, and those secrets got him killed.”

I could hear my mother’s heavy breathing and her voice broke when she spoke her next words.

“Oh Nevaeh, your father had his reasons.”

“Well, burn them, or read them, or whatever, but I don’t want them. The last thing I want is to read conversations Dad thought he was having with someone so powerful, but couldn’t even save him.”

"Honey… everything has a purpose… a reason," my mom's voice whined out.

It was like sandpaper being rubbed on my skin. I hyperventilated. No, not now, damn it! Come on!

"I have to go. Love you," I gasped out before I quickly tapped the end button and leaned back against my worn-out couch.

Letters. To me and God. What a joke. I coaxed my breathing back to normal and tossed my phone on the table as it began vibrating again. It rang three more times before my mom finally gave up. I drank that bottle and then grabbed another one, which had conveniently been stashed in the back of my fridge.

~ ~ ~

I woke up with a pounding headache and immediately padded to the fridge to grab a bottle of water. Then downed four aspirin. Looking down, I noticed six missed calls from my mom and one from Nate. The house was so quiet without two toddlers running around because Nate had taken our four-year-old and six-year-old to a baseball game overnight. Having them running around was getting more difficult with how much energy I was putting into social media.

Being active on TikTok, YouTube, Instagram, and Facebook was bringing in a couple thousand extra a month, but it took a lot of time and consistent posting. If not, I was just another bland face, empty and unimportant to watch, follow, or pay attention to. It had to be entertaining. It had to be professional. It had to be fresh and new. Every. Single. Day. If not multiple times a day.

Remembering Nate's missed call and ignoring my mother's, I quickly dialed his number to check in.

"Hey, how are the kids?" my voice came out soft.

CHAPTER TWO

Stagnant

The sound of our kids' giggles and tumbling footsteps echoed through the phone before I heard Nate's response. Despite myself, I could feel the tears brimming over. What was wrong with me?

"Doing good! How're the uploads coming?"

"Oh, um, to be honest, I haven't done as much as I should. My mom called. She said she found some more of my dad's stuff."

"Nevey, the whole point of me taking the kids was so you would have time to get things done. You said you were going to pre-post for the next month. That was our agreement."

My skin prickled, and I pinched my lips together. Didn't he hear what I said about my dad? Why didn't he see? I sighed and pushed my growing frustration aside like I always did. "I know, I know. I'm on it. Just take your time. I'll be done by the time you get home."

"I hope so. I really hate when you say you're going to do things and don't."

Anger pulsed behind my eyes. I rubbed my temples forcefully. "Yeah, I know. It's getting done, okay?"

"Alright. I'll talk to you later."

The phone clicked, and I stared at it in wonder. Are you kidding me? I looked around the room. My dream house, large and open concept with pristine and expensive appliances. A Pinterest home, but a complete mess. The kitchen was enormous and in shambles because I hadn't cleaned since before they left yesterday. Clothes were spread around the room, the floor was littered with crumbs and dirt, and the sink was full of dishes from the breakfast I'd made the previous morning. I didn't even want to see the kids' rooms.

A cold sweat spread across the back of my neck and the palms of my hands. My headache was still pulsing with a rhythmic beat that was irritating. I wiped my hands on my sweatpants. Holy crap, I'm not even dressed yet! Come on Nevey, get it together.

I padded to our bedroom, the bed still disheveled, despite it now approaching afternoon. Laundry was piled up on both our sides because I hadn't started it. I sighed and my gaze bounced around, a stream of overwhelming thoughts coursing through my mind. I drank again, instead of getting what I needed done. What was wrong with me?

A scratching issued from the bathroom, and I tilted my head at a soft meow. I walked to the bathroom and threw my hands up in defeat. Stupid. You are so dang stupid. Lexie, our family cat, sat while she looked at me with her black cat brows furrowed and her slanted eyes squinted. She slowly slid her food bowl across the floor with a smoky gray paw. The noise scraped against my skull, and I huffed loudly while again throwing my hands in the air.

"Are you kidding me? What else! What else needs to get done in this stupid house? What else is wrong? What else do I have to do before everyone gets home?"

The sound of my voice sent the cat skittering away while meowing loudly in disgust. Her tail flicked around the door, and I spun to see her move under the bed. Good job Nevey.

I chewed on my lip and took a deep breath to calm the rising anxiety. The miniature Jack Daniel's bottles I had sitting on the top shelf in my bathroom for decoration were looking really appealing. I clicked open my phone to distract myself for a second. One hundred and sixty-eight notifications from a gym post I'd put up yesterday. I looked at it for a second and smiled. The tight-fitted yoga shorts and sports bra I had worn was highlighted on my screen. I scanned through comments and poured out some cat food into the bowl. There were already over three hundred comments and almost three thousand likes.

My body tingled and elation crashed into every cell like a wave. It was intoxicating, the feeling of so many eyes on me. Oh boy, Nate's gonna kill me when he sees this! At least I had the excuse that it's making us money. Finally satisfied and the urge to drink again chased away, I looked at the bowl of food.

"Lexie," I whispered, drawing out her name while I rattled it and ambled to the bed. I bent down, my knees pushing into the soft cream carpet, and lifted our thick beige comforter. "Lexie, I'm sorry. You can come out, no more scary monster Mom."

Lexie gave a hesitant meow, and I continued to slowly shake the bowl until she finally made her way out. Her eyes were pinched in an anxious but also accusing way that shouldn't be possible for a cat. "What? I'm having a bad day. Actually, it's been a terrible year. I'm sorry, okay?" Her meow of a response was a dismissal, so I set the food down and pushed up from the floor to finally get ready.

My phone vibrated as I was picking out comfortable gym clothes. I clicked the phone subconsciously and looked back at Lexie who was now munching on her food happily.

"What, Mom?" I shouldn't be so mean, but the woman was persistent and never shut up about God. I loved her to death, but not everything was about him.

"That's not a way to greet your mother. You know I gave birth to you? In the car on the way to the hospital. I carried you for ten months, Nevaeh. Then I hemorrhaged and almost died there in the car. God saved me because He knew you needed me. He told me to name you Nevaeh right there. We had to replace the seat after that because there was so much blood."

I rolled my eyes. My mother was notorious for expressing how amazing it was that she gave birth in the car. She continued to prattle on, and I quickly put my phone on speaker so I could finish getting dressed.

"Then your Dad ended up wanting to sell the car, and God blessed us with a brand new one that would fit all four of you! Before that, we were squeezing your twin brothers into a seat so I could fit your car seat."

"I'm well aware Mom. I've heard the story a million times."

"God is so good, Nevaeh. Why can't you see that?"

I picked my phone back up and shut off the speaker. "If God is so wonderful, Mom, why did He take Dad? If He's so great, why didn't He cure his cancer? If God is so great, Mom, why did Mathew drown in the pool when I was eight? If God is so great, Mom, and you're so faithful, why is Mark still an addict? There is no God."

"Don't you dare, Nevaeh. Don't you dare talk like that. We are human. We are sinners. I don't always know or understand, but God is forever and will always be good."

"God is dead, Mom. As dead as Dad. Cold and rotting in the grave."

My mom's gasp sent a tremor of self-hatred rolling through my body. Good going, Nevey. It was temporary and gone in a flash, but it was still enough to make me nauseated. I pulled back my hair in a ponytail and shook out my body and one of my arms while still holding the phone with the other. Time to work off some steam, apparently. My attention had already moved away from my mom's prattling, but her quiet voice sent a chill through me and pushed my focus back to the conversation.

"God is silent. God is far from dead. Your lack of faith is going to cause more hardship in your life than you need to go through, Nevey. He is watching, waiting, and about to make moves in your life that are going to pull you back to Him, whether or not you like it."

"Mom, I respect your resilience and determination, but all God has ever done to me is take. If He loves us so much, why does He want to control us? I will never believe in something that wants to do that to me."

"I know you don't understand, honey, but someday you will. I miss your father terribly, just like you. My heart will forever be broken. I can't pretend to understand why He chose not to heal your father, but the cracks in you are beginning to show."

I sighed heavily. There were always cracks in me. If I didn't know I was human and had proof of baby pictures, I wouldn't be surprised to find out I was a porcelain doll that had been broken and glued back together.

"Well, God is going to be waiting a long time. I'm sorry, Mom, but He's just not real to me. Anyways, I have to go. I need to get the house cleaned and do some pre-posting before Nate and the kids get home. Otherwise, Nate's gonna have a cow."

I grabbed the vacuum mop so I could quickly clean up the floor as my phone began to vibrate and pulled it away from my ear to see a text message. Mom continued on her rampage as I looked at it. The gym picture was on display across my screen with a very upset message from Nate. My heart plummeted in my stomach, and a stone of dread replaced it. I knew he would be mad, but I wasn't expecting this response.

"Mom, I have to go," I cut her off mid-sentence before I hung up so I could open the message fully.

CHAPTER THREE

Cracks

His message made me want to throw up. The world tilted and the sound of my heartbeat filled my ears.

"GREAT! JUST WHAT I WANTED TO SEE, COMMENTS ABOUT MY WIFE ON SOCIAL MEDIA. THIS IS THE FIFTH TIME. NEVAEH, I'M DONE. I WANT A DIVORCE."

My hands shook as the black letters embedded themselves in my mind. A tattoo on the folds of my brain. Cheap. Worthless. It kept repeating in my head like a messed-up mantra. We'd had issues before with certain things I posted, but I never thought anything of it. I looked around me and the tears brimmed over- thick and salty. They soaked my face. My eyes darted around, looking for something… anything to hold onto as my world tilted off it's axis.

Partially blinded by my tears and my head swimming, I sped to our wedding photo sitting on my bedside table. I grasped a hold of it like a lifeline. My beaming husband with crow black hair and hazel eyes. The flecks of green highlighted by our photographers' incredible editing skills. The freckles dotting his cheeks and above his forehead. My mother always called freckles heaven's kisses when I was growing up.

My mouse brown hair, braided into a curled side ponytail was plain. My pale blue eyes were even more plain compared to his. He was a dream, and I don't know when I became such a dumpster fire to disregard it. How lucky I was to have him. My body began to shake. Rolling sobs. I didn't realize till I threw the picture and it shattered against the floor.

Who do I call? Who do I talk to? My brain spun. Divorce. He said divorce. No woman empowerment. No; "good job, babe, for working your butt off. For bringing in extra money." No recognizing my pain. No asking if I was ok. When did he stop caring? When did he stop seeing me?

My brain pinged from thought to thought. Alone. Worthless. No one can love you. Ugly. Why does everything bad always happen to me? The anger began to rise. The feeling of fire boiled low in my stomach, the heat colored my cheeks. I quickly texted one word.

"F. I. N. E."

"Happy Mr. All Powerful God? YOU DON'T EXIST! If You are so great, then why don't You come? Show me You're real. Comfort Your sobbing child, Father," My voice came out, laced with venom. My hands clinched into fists, and I looked down. I'd slowly made my way to the picture. Glass pieces surrounded it. I leaned down and looked at it with a dying heart. The color of my tanned skin peeled slightly back in a thick line, revealing the white because a shard of glass had cut it. I rubbed my thumb against it. Someone cackled low in the back of my head.

The light flickered off the shards as I began to pick them up. One nicked me as I stuffed them into my hand. "Ow!" I looked down. Blood bubbled up and dripped down my finger. I stuffed it in my mouth and when I pulled it out, a small amount was still there. The way I pulled my finger out made the shape of it look like a cross. I snorted at myself and rolled my eyes.

"That all You got, Mr. Almighty?"

The cackling in my head got louder. I finished picking up the picture and the shards of glass and placed them on the picture. Divorce. No sense in keeping the picture then.

My phone vibrated. I didn't realize I was still holding it while picking up glass shards. My best friend Skylar's sea foam green eyes and red curly hair was splayed on the screen.

"Hey Sky, I umm, I can't talk right now."

"Oh honey, what's going on? I can hear the crying in your voice."

I took a breath and wiped my eyes. Acting. I'm good at that. All my posts showed that. I plastered a smile on my face to make it more real, despite my quivering lips, before responding.

"Nothing, I'm doing great! Did you see the traffic on my last post?

She didn't respond for a second, and I'm sure she was chewing on her lip, thinking over if I was lying or not.

"I'm worried about you, Nevey. Something feels off. It feels like something's brewing."

"Well, aren't you a nosey Nelly?"

"I'm your best friend. We grew up together. I earned that right when I punched Drake in the face after we found out he cheated on you. Thank God, I was so happy when that paperwork was signed."

Divorced. Right before I met Nate. Four divorces within ten years. I ticked them off in my head, the names forming a disgusting list.

"What number was he?"

"Four," I say lightly, my voice breaking.

"That's right. You had Paul, always full of himself. Then Greg, who wouldn't even let you buy twenty-dollar shoes, and Edward. That dude was crazy, he was angry, lazy, and jealous all the time. See, that's my problem. You never listen to me, but you always jump in the lake and then drown. I mean, at least you waited two years with Nate, and he has all the good stuff."

"I'm already drowning," I mumbled before putting my hand over my mouth. Shit, Nevey, you shouldn't have said that.

"Huh?"

"Nothing Sky, I'm doing great. I promise."

"All right, well, when we gonna have another Chai Latte night? I need some content for Chai Addicts."

I furrowed my brows. "You know, you've been getting a lot of hatred for that name. Being an addict and all. How long has it been now?"

"Four year's next week! Not a drop." She popped her lips together for emphasis and I couldn't help but smile.

"I am so dang proud of you, girl!"

"Thanks, lovely. All right. I'll let you go."

I could hear her rustling something around. I wiped my face again, the tears almost dry, and cocked my head to the side. "What are you doing?"

"Oh nothing, just got back from the store. Making some popcorn for Stella, Sorral, and Rory. Justin wanted to watch a movie with the kids tonight. You know how determined he gets when there's a new movie out. Wanna come over?"

"Oh no, that's okay. Nate's coming home with the kids today, and I still need to clean the house. It's a disaster."

"Do you need help? I'm only five minutes away- a fifteen-minute walk. I could use the exercise."

"Eh, I'm just gonna put on some headphones and get all my pre-posting done." I didn't want her to see me like this. I didn't want her to know this would be my fifth divorce. I didn't want her to know how useless I was. How no one could love me with all my malfunctions. Not even my mother could tolerate me without trying to shove her God down my throat.

"All right, how does Saturday sound for a posting Chai day then?"

"Sounds good."

"Love you bestie. You would tell me if something was wrong, right?"

"Yes bestie. You're my sister, I'm not lying. Love you to the moon and beyond. Bye!"

I hung up before she could say anything else. The tears began to roll down my face again and I couldn't stop them. I clinched my jaw and tossed the remnants of the picture I was still clutching in the trash. Then, I walked to the bathroom, climbed on the counter and grabbed all six small bottles of Jack displayed. Three in each hand. I stood there, my body reflected in the mirror, on the counter. I stared at myself, and slowly opened each bottle. I stared at my empty face as I drank each one and let them clatter into the sink. I stood there on the counter, as my head grazed the ceiling.

"You are pathetic, Nevaeh. Your mom cursed you. Seriously. Who names their child Heaven backwards? Blessing my ass."

A knock issued from my front door, and I spun on the counter, almost toppling off. What now? Oh God, please don't let that be the kids and Nate already.

CHAPTER FOUR

Falling apart

The knocking continued. It was getting more insistent. I debated hiding in my closet to wait for the warming belly effect of the alcohol, but the pounding got harder.

"Coming. Just a second," I shouted.

I jumped down from the counter and ambled down the short hallway to my front room. The entire house was cream carpet. Most people hated carpet, especially with kids, but I didn't enjoy walking on cold floors. Nate hads tried to convince me. Being the manager of the local grocery store meant we definitely had the money.

I threw the door open as someone's muffled voice tried to penetrate the thick wood. A hand sat poised in the air.

"Mom, what are you doing?"

"You have now hung up on me twice and not answered when I called. I presumed either you were dead, being killed, or kidnapped."

I threw my head back and blew my cheeks out dramatically.

"Ugh… hey sis," Rebekah, my forty-year-old sister's voice, said.

"I brought reinforcements," my mother said.

"Reinforcements?"

"Well, your brothers are on their way. This is a very serious family matter."

"Malachi and Mark? I thought Mark was in rehab?"

My mother tsked and smoothed her delicately styled hair. She rolled her eyes. "Yes Nevey, he is in rehab, now if you would keep in contact with your family for more than a few minutes at a time, and we didn't have to see your life through social media, you would know Mark graduated from his program, and now he is on a behavioral health program three days a week."

I snorted. "I don't talk to any of you because you're all crazy. How many programs has he been in the last year? How many has he gotten kicked out of?"

Rebekah stepped around our mother protectively, her sky-blue eyes identical to our mother's, formed small slits. She took a defensive stance and our mother peered around her innocently, her hands planted firmly on her full hips.

"I don't know what your problem is, or why you have blacklisted the family. But you're going to shut up and listen."

My eyes widened. Rebekah was usually quiet and kept to herself. Her hair was always cut short and curled to complement her face. The woman was gorgeous. I mean for Pete sakes, she still looked thirty.

My stomach was beginning to warm, and I giggled. They both looked at me, and my mother's eyebrows rose. She stepped forward and slightly pushed Rebekah out of the way.

She was shorter than both of us, my sister standing at 5'8, and I stood at 5'7. Mother was only 5'4, but she held more authority than both of us combined. She leaned toward me, her beautiful face tipped upward. Why did everyone look ten or fifteen years younger in my family?

"Funny for you to curl your lip at your brother-" She sniffed me and I involuntarily took a step back, letting go of the door. Taking it as an invitation, they both stepped through quickly, like vultures attacking a scrap of roadkill and slammed the door. "When you have been drinking so heavily, I can smell wine and whiskey on your breath and clothes."

I scoffed. "Okay, Mom, you might have a wonderful smell, but I'm sorry. You can't smell the difference between alcohol."

"Did you forget your father was an alcoholic? For fifteen years, he struggled with alcoholism and depression. For fifteen years, he snuck different ways of getting the alcohol he wanted, and I smelled it all. Addiction isn't a joke. It isn't something to sneer at and be disgusted by."

"What? Is this an intervention?" I looked at them smugly. My eyes bounced back and forth between them. The small buzz was burning away from the anger that pulsed through me. I tried to chase it down, to stop it from leaving, but it sped away. Great. No more buzz. My sister was tapping on her phone. She used a hand to fold a piece of hair behind her ear. The gesture just pissed me off as I took in her perfect clothes. "You are always so perfect, aren't you, Rebekah? The perfect child. Never any mistakes from Rebekah."

Her eyes slowly moved up, those crystal blues taking me in. Pity. She had pity deep in the depths. She smiled sadly and shoved her phone slowly in her pocket. Our gazes locked for a few seconds as she clasped her hands together. She took me in, making me feel uncomfortable. Satisfied, and still not saying a word, her gaze shifted and moved around my house. Oh shit. It's a disaster!

"Despite what you may think, Nevaeh. Despite what you may see, I am far from perfect. But right now, my perfect butt is going to get to work and clean your house." Without another word, she walked over to the broom cupboard and grabbed my broom.

Our mother looked up at her and smiled warmly before looking back at me. The same look of pity crossed her face. I clinched my fists. I wanted to punch something.

"This isn't an intervention, Nevaeh. This is your family coming to help you," my mother said. She looked at a perfectly manicured nail before she walked past me toward the kitchen. Giving a small smile, she grasped my hand as she elegantly drifted past and squeezed.

"Get out. Get out of my house. I don't want you here," I whispered, shaking.

"No."

"Get out," I said more firmly.

CHAPTER FIVE

Enough

I looked at my mom and pulled as much hostility into my stance as I could fathom. Every bit of me wanted to grab her shoulders and shake her, the saint of a woman. Her faith never faltered, and I hated her for it.

"No. I'm not leaving, and neither is Rebekah. We're going to clean your house. We're going to sit down and talk. We're going to be a family for once."

"I don't want you here. I want you out. All you're gonna talk about is God and I am so damn fed up with God talk. Just get out."

"Nevaeh Serenity. God may be at my center, but I am smart enough to recognize that a conversation involving God isn't always what a person needs." She ruffled her hair and placed her hands on her hips. Her lips were pinched together and she was glaring at me in a way only a mother could. "Now, are you going to help me or just stand there gawking like a fish?"

My eyes widened. I opened and closed my fists before blowing out a thick breath of air. "Fine," I mumbled before moving forward to grab the vacuum mop I'd left in the middle of the room. Well, I guess music was off the table. I watched my mom sidelong as I unwound the vacuum. She walked up to my sister and began helping her do the dishes. They mumbled to each other, the bubbles filled the sink as the faucet sprayed out tendrils of steaming water.

I shook my head and focussed on plugging the vacuum in. Before I could start, another knock rang through the house. I frowned; the cord still draped in my hand. "Is that Mark and Malachi?"

My sister and mother looked at each other, Rebekah held a dishtowel. My mother was elbow deep with suds on her arms and held a plate. Rebekah nodded as our mother shrugged. I threw my hands in the air. I guess it was becoming my new thing. “Don’t worry, I’ll get it.”

Rebekah chortled and shook her head.

I rolled my eyes while I made a show of stomping to my door. “Welcome to the shit show… where family is a pain and messes are required. Can I help you?” I said with a fake smile plastered on my face as I threw the door open.

“Well, you’re not as nice as I remember,” the low timber of my brother said as he shoved a large box into my hands. I stumbled back a step before catching myself.

“Ooof, what the-”

“Nice to see you too, sis.” His rich brown eyes twinkled in a way I hadn’t seen them do in a long time.

The last time I remembered seeing him, he was at least fifteen pounds underweight, was high off his gird, and had stolen my mother's necklace worth six thousand dollars. A necklace that was paired with a matching set of rings my sister and I were supposed to get when our mother passed. The necklace was supposed to go to the firstborn, Matthew, but because he was six feet in the ground, it would go to his twin brother Malachi.

I adjusted myself. The box was heavy. "Are you bringing me body parts now?"

"I mean, you could technically say that." He flicked his mouse brown hair out of his eyes, hair identical to my own, but he had a dusting of freckles littered across his full cheeks. My God, my brother had full cheeks. They weren't sunken in like an addict usually was.

"I swear Mark… that's not funny."

"Oh, calm yourself. Can I come inside? Or are you gonna leave me on the doorstep?"

"That depends. Are you gonna steal priceless heirlooms?"

"Nevaeh," my mother's voice lashed out like a whip.

Mark and I spun toward her. I caught him rolling his eyes.

"What? Did you ever get that necklace back?" I asked while raising an eyebrow.

"Actually, yes she did. Last month," he said as he shoved past me. I stumbled backwards in shock.

"Wha...what?"

"I told you, if you would spend more than a few minutes on the phone, a few minutes not talking or worrying about yourself, you would find out some pretty intriguing things about your family," my mother said.

Rebekah nodded her head in agreement. They had finished putting the dishes away and Rebekah was munching on my peanut brittle.

"Um,.. a follower sent me that... you didn't want to ask?"

She snorted before responding. "When have you ever asked me before taking something?"

Ok, touché. I couldn't argue there. I didn't respond, but her smirk was enough to know she was right.

"Good lord Nevaeh, do you enjoy living in a pig pin?" The crack of a can ensued, and I looked over at Mark while he stared at me. He took a long sip of a coke and grabbed a handful of peanut brittle from the small tub.

I clinched my jaw. “You are the most annoying insufferable jackass I have ever met.”

“What? Can’t afford a housekeeper with your publicity?”

“Mom-”

I swear, it was like we’re kids all over again. Mark, always the one poking fun, Rebekah rolling her eyes, and my mother choking on laughter as she used a cleaning rag and spray bottle to wipe the counter over and over. Once Malachi was here, if he would even come, I would never survive.

Malachi and Mark complemented each other, even though they were two years apart, they acted like twins. It’d been that way ever since Mathew passed away.

“Mom can’t save you, Nevey, you have to save yourself.” Mark shrugged and looked at the box. He smiled knowingly.

“What’s in the box, Mark?” I said, my focus moved by his obvious attention to it.

"I dunno- maybe you should open it and find out."

I looked at it suspiciously, knowing my crack pot brother, it would probably be a dead cat or a spider.

"You know. What is it?"

"Oh, you got me. Hmm… dusty bones?" My mother laughed and clasped her hand over her mouth to hide it. Her cheeks were flushed, and she had wiped the same spot eight times. I was counting as he talked.

"Come on Nevey, we all wanna know what's in the weightlifting box."

"Weightlifting box?"

"Oh, Nevey, always a little slow… you know, cuz it's heavy." He winked again; a beam spread across his face. The dimple on his one cheek popped out. "Open it, open it, open it," Mark chanted.

I held my breath and set the box down. I was gonna be so pissed if something jumped on me. I vowed right there to send him back to the rehab, cut into little pieces, and shoved uncomfortably into that box.

CHAPTER SIX

Mistakes

I snorted at the thought of shoving my 6'2 brother, even in pieces, into the box. Maybe his head? Goodness gracious, I was losing my mind.

"What're you giggling about?" Mark asked.

I looked up and grinned. "Oh, that's for me to know," I said, and winked.

Both his eyebrows shot into his hairline, and he took a step back while he raised his hands. I looked back at my sister, who nodded to the broom she'd gotten out before she helped my mom with the dishes instead. That was so like her, to start something before she abandoned it because our mother was doing something else.

It really wasn't a big deal, but everything about her had always irritated me. She was our mother's pride and joy, the golden child, and she knew it.

"If you think I'm gonna clean, you're sadly mistaken, Bek's."

"Mark, this is a family affair. Get the broom, or a dust rag and get to work," our mother said. She glared at him before clicking her tongue. She looked at the box, then me, then the broom, and last, her gaze slid back to my brother. She threw the dishtowel down and walked around the counter. "Where is your duster and extra rags, Nevaeh?" she asked as she placed her hands on her hips.

I knew I wouldn't win, and to be honest, who's to say I didn't want the help? I sighed and looked at the box longingly. Usually when Mark made jokes, there was an underlying reason laced behind it. I shook my head in defeat. "It's in the broom closet Rebekah was in when you first got here. There's a shelf dedicated to soft rags and a bucket with cleaning supplies."

"Perfect. Mark, you do the dusting, Rebekah, you finish cleaning the kitchen. I'll clean the bathrooms. Nevaeh, I want you to put that box in your room, put a load of laundry on, lord knows you probably haven't done it in several weeks. Then I want you to vacuum mop."

"It's only been a little over a couple weeks," I said. My voice came out more whiney than I intended, and I kicked myself internally.

"Regardless, I'm sure there's a mountain of clothes in that room." I gritted my teeth and glared at her as she tilted her head to the side. "Am I wrong?"

"Nope," I said while stooping over to pick up the box. Rebekah had already grabbed the bucket of cleaning supplies. She placed it delicately on the kitchen counter and started ruffling through it. I shifted my weight and looked at the box again. Feeling eyes on me, I looked over at Mark, who was grinning and still sipping on the coke.

"What're you lookin at?" I said, as my nose wrinkled and my face scrunched in disgust.

"I don't know but it's weird looking."

I huffed out a breath while I shook my head and began to stomp down my hall. Rebekah was chuckling under her breath. Our mother was chastising Mark to get busy. When I reached my room, I almost took a seat to secretly open the box, but a knock rang through my house again. Good lord, how many people were going to come today? "Can one of you answer that?" I quickly set the box on my bed and tripped my way out the door.

My gosh Nevey, for a social media icon, you are one heck of a klutz.

"Who is it?" I asked as I walked down the hall. I had my phone in my back pocket and took it out as I walked. My post was now up to fifteen thousand likes and over a thousand comments. My heart shuttered in excitement. That temporary high, just like my buzz, was chased away as I realized Nate still hadn't messaged me.

"Well, hello little mouse," a familiar voice pushed out.

I stopped in the middle of my short hallway. My hand drifted down to my side, still holding my phone. The smile that had already been slipping immediately turned into a tight-lipped line. I hadn't seen Malachi in eight years. He was the oldest out of all of us, and he was also the tallest. His hair was a shocking blonde, as if someone had captured the sun's light and weaved them into smooth strands before placing them perfectly on his head. When Mathew had passed away, something inside him snapped. He became a rabid lion. Being ten years older than me, I was easy prey.

"How nice of you to show up," I said while biting my lip. He had our father's moss green eyes. They looked almost sad.

"I know," he said. Those two words were enough to make my lip quiver.

I cleared my throat and pushed myself to stand up taller. "Alright, happy? Everyone is here, all nice and cozy. What now?"

"Nevaeh," Mark started, but I cut him off.

"It's just Nevey, Mark. Even all my social media says that."

"My, my little mouse, your rash attitude hasn't changed," Malachi spit out. His eyes squinted at me. I looked at him. My face was a marble statue. My lips were pursed, my eyes in small slits with my hand squeezing my phone.

"I'm not a mouse, I am a grown ass woman, and I will be damned if you don't start treating me like one. I haven't seen you for years, and the first thing you decide to do is approach me, in my house, by the way, with hostility? You can get the hell out. I didn't ask for this. I didn't ask for you to be here." I was rambling, and I knew it, but I couldn't stop.

"Neva.. I mean, Nevey. It's the anniversary," Mark cut in. He looked between us. His usual teasing expression replaced by a dim light. Pity. Just like my mother and Rebekah.

"Wha…what?"

"It's been twenty-five years," Rebekah said under her breath.

Our mother was looking at all of us with concern. Her eyes had softened.

"It's been twenty-five years and you're still blaming yourself," my mother chimed in.

I heard Malachi whisper, "She *should* still blame herself."

CHAPTER SEVEN

It is done

Oh no. I could feel the tears brimming over. The sobs building. Too much. Why? Why was everything happening? Why did everyone hate me? Why did everyone leave me? It's just like Daddy. I killed him too. If I'd told Mama about the Dr's visit. He said it was routine, but I heard through the door. He made me promise not to tell anyone. I never did, even after he died.

I was a child again, waiting for the blows from my brother. I shoved my hands over my ears, trembling, waiting for them all to yell at me in disgust. So they're here for this. To finally say how much they hated me. I looked up at the sound of my mom's voice.

"Malachi Paraclete. Look at your sister! Look what you've done to her!" She thrust out her hand before shuffling toward me. She delicately took my hands and pulled them away from my ears, like she used to do when I was a child and overstimulated. She would hold my hands and rock with me. Humming some song to chase away the demons.

She kissed my cheek and patted my hands. I couldn't help myself as I leaned into her touch. I didn't realize I felt so alone. Why? I shouldn't. On social media, I was very popular.

"It has been twenty-five years. Your sister was eight years old. She had no knowledge that he was drunk. She ran away to hide because he and his friends were chasing and tickling her. You and Mathew decided-"

"She shoved him in the pool!" Malachi shouted. His hands clinched while a vein pulsed in his forehead.
I stepped back and looked over my shoulder. Run. Run. Run. I killed him. I killed him. My fingers were trembling and my mind was a blinking billboard of negative thoughts. There was so much shame and disgust inside me that I wanted to scream.

My mother tensed and raised herself to her full height. Not that it was much. Her eyes flashed; her face pinched in hostility I'd never seen before. "You will not interrupt me again, young man! Enough is enough. It is done. God had a plan, a purpose for his death. You and Matthew wanted to have that party. Twenty-five years, Malachi. You were eighteen, and you continue to put responsibility that isn't hers on her shoulders. Has she not paid enough from your wrath?"

"He was playing with her! It was a joke!"

"And you were both drunk," Rebekah said flatly. She looked at me. She shook her head.

Her gaze dropped, and she ran a hand through her short hair.

I continued to shake, the bitter taste of stomach acid on my tongue. That day was an image tattooed on my brain. For the first time in many years, I could feel the walls closing in. They continued to argue back and forth, Mark finally jumping in, but I couldn't hear what they were saying. My head was spinning, and I felt dizzy. A cool black blanket was spreading across my shoulders. No, no, no, not now.

I spun on my heal, the taste of salt and vomit on the back of my tongue. I heard Rebekah shouting. My mother's fingertips grazed me, but I slid from her touch. I ran. I didn't know where, I just knew I needed to get away. I made it to my bedroom and Mark was close on my heels but slammed the door in his face and quickly pushed the lock into place. I collapsed. My knees hit the fluffy cream carpet hard, but if it hurt, I didn't feel it.

I sagged against the ground, sobs wracking my body and making it hard to breathe. I held my breath, trying to grasp control. Be still. It was a small voice in my head, but it didn't sound like me. Be still. It said again. Huh? My voice said.

"Wonderful. Now I'm having breakdowns and talking to myself. Just great."

Be still. It said again, more urgently.

I whimpered. Those two words were now a continuous mantra. Part of me wanted them to shut up, while the other part was sighing in relief. They repeated over and over, but as I sat there on my knees, still and sobbing, I calmed. The hammering of my heart slowed and the tang of fear dissipated, replaced instead by a calm I hadn't felt since I was a child. My chest was tight. I was still panicked, but there was something on the edge of my inner turmoil. A peace.

"Nevaeh! Nevey, please, it's not your fault. We all know that. Malachi… well, Malachi is Malachi," Mark said through the door.

I ignored him as he continued to talk through the door. I could imagine his lips pressed against it like he used to do when we were children.

My brother, the peacekeeper. Who finally snapped and turned to drugs. The one who kept it together for everyone else suddenly split open like a jar of peanut butter. He'd been through so many rehab programs that I had lost track. Every time he overdosed, when I was a child, our mother's screams would be defining as he walked through the door. Still alive thanks to the Narcan the officers or EMT's had given him.

As if in a trance, I pushed up from the floor. The repeated words were gone. Tears rolled down my face without a sound. A new word repeated in my head now. Journal. Over and over. I spun slowly, unfocused. My brother pounded on the door and shouted through it. I could feel the panic, as if he thought I was like him. As if I was going to do something stupid.

I looked down and stopped moving toward the bed. My phone was lighting up. Nate was calling. I ignored him, too. Instead, I popped open my screen. I hadn't pre-posted as much as I wanted, but there were a few posts pending. My head continued to repeat the word journal, but I ignored that, too. I tried to get a fix… to feel better from the comments on my social media posts. The lines were blurry, and they didn't make me feel better.

I heard my doorbell. No one used that, unless it was friends that weren't close. Muffled voices, then silence again. My brother had finally given up. His desperation gone. Good riddance. I didn't need his pity. I was used to being on my own. I didn't need anyone. Everyone always left me anyway.

Journal, the voice in my head said again. I was tired of talking to myself.

"Shut up," I said.

I was busy. Too busy scanning through my phone. Hundreds of posts, thousands of comments, thousands of likes. Posts of inspiration, of not letting life knock you down, of not needing God, of being a badass woman, a badass mom, concurring anything in your life.

Journal, the voice said more urgently. It wasn't panicked, but something about it sent chills down my spine.

What journal? What do you want? I asked myself. Good lord, someone is gonna commit me. I clicked off my posts. Self-hatred spread like a nasty wildfire, so I put my phone in my back pocket. I didn't want to, but something told me I needed to.

"Nevaeh, open the door. Come on. Malachi left. Mom is beside herself," Rebekah said.

I looked over my shoulder, chewed on my lip and kicked the carpet.

"Nevey, did you hear me? Get out here. Mom is slaving away by herself."

I spun, but something stopped me from walking to the door. Instead, I stood there listening to the frustrated complaints of Rebekah. She continued on before she finally gave up like Mark had. I stared at the door for several seconds before I turned back to the box.

I walked up to it slowly but was stopped again as my hands grazed against the soft cardboard. They came to rest on the slick tape. It felt like seconds passed, but with how long Mark had stood at my door, begging, pleading, and muffled panic, followed by

Rebekah and her frustrated cries, it must have been a long time. My mother's voice sent a ping of pain through my chest. I sucked in a large breath of air.

"Nevaeh Serenity, you can't keep running. You can't keep hiding. We don't blame you."

I could hear her crying. Her soft crying matched my own silent tears. Tears that didn't seem to dry.

"Mama, I can't," my voice was low. Mangled and broken, like I was.

"Oh baby, I know it's scary." I heard my mother's body press against the door before it slid slowly down.

"This was never supposed to happen. This isn't what I wanted for you. Please come out so we can talk."

"I can't. I can't. I can't," I said, almost talking to myself.

"Ok honey, we will be here when you're ready. I'm sorry baby girl. I'm sorry for everything, I'm sorry for leaving that night. I'm sorry your daddy and I got so mad at you.

I'm sorry we didn't see how Malachi was treating you. I love you so much."

Her last words were dead on my ears as my chest clinched.

CHAPTER EIGHT

When everything falls apart

I must have been broken. I was hurting, but I didn't care if I was hurting anyone else. My family was sitting there, cleaning my house, and I'd barricaded myself in my room. Not to mention that I was obviously going insane repeating the word "journal" when I hadn't owned a journal since I was seven. The stupid thing was neon pink with a lock and key. Rebekah had dangled it above the toilette shouting about my crush before accidently dropping it in. I remember screaming at the top of my lungs for two minutes straight, till she promised I could

have her desert for the next week if I didn't tell our mom what had happened.
I looked back at the box while I tapped my ears with open palms. Are you terrified of a box, Nevey?

"Alright Mr. Box, no more distractions. You're gonna open up and show me the bones Mark was talking about," I said as I lurched forward.

Again, my hand found the slick tape. I ripped it off quickly and jumped back. No surprises yet. The tape came off easily and stuck to my hand. I shook my hand, but it held on. I took it off and stuck it to the bed. When I opened the tabs, I expected a foul smell or something to jump out. Nothing happened. I peered inside and almost fell over. My eyes widened with surprise.

The smell of worn paper assaulted my nose. I hated that smell. I remembered it though because Sky loved collecting old leather-bound books. She had a library dedicated to them. Oh the joy of being wealthy and the ability to spend your money on random stuff.

Peering closer, I think my eyebrows disappeared into my hairline. They were journals. Journals a few years old. At least eighteen of them, if not more.

Journal, my mind said softly, a sigh against my imagination. I pulled one out. All different colored leather. Different blues and browns, swollen from the ink in the pages. Ruffled. The one I grabbed had my name scrolled across it and the date I turned thirty. I opened it.

"He wrote letters to you, and God," I heard my mom say during our phone conversation. So, she didn't burn them. They weren't just letters… this was an account of my entire life. Or at least the year I turned thirty. Somewhere around when I was divorcing my third or fourth husband.

The writing from my father was smooth and firm. Mark wasn't kidding when he said it was technically full of dusty bones. I scrolled writing I hadn't seen in several months across the page. I pulled in a breath. It caught in my throat and I gasped. I spun and slid down to the floor again. Thank God for the soft carpet. Every detail was written out as I flipped through the pages. Every phone conversation. Every lunch date that year was written out in small, dedicated writing. Love poured into those pages. I couldn't explain it, but I could feel it.

I don't know how long I sat there, crying silently as I read it all. The faint smell of my father's cologne was stuck to the pages. I would have stayed there, but a knock issued at my door as my phone vibrated again.

"Hello?" I said as my voice broke.

"Nevey?"

I bit my lip to stop the shudder in my voice.

"Yeah?" I said. A broken question.

"Are you crying?" Nate's voice was tense, but he didn't sound like he cared.

"Um, it's just been a tough day."

"Oh, well, I'm staying here one more night with the kiddos. Is that alright with you? They wanted to go to the zoo, but we didn't have time today. I don't have to go to the store, so I figured we could go to the zoo for a few hours."

I plastered a smile on my face and wiped my eyes while I snapped the journal shut. “Yeah sure. That sounds like a brilliant plan.”

“Well, don’t you sound enthusiastic?”

“There’s just a lot going on here, Nate.” My hand squeezed against the phone. The old Nate would have asked me if I was okay, the one who still loved me would have known I was hiding something. I swallowed my tongue to keep from saying something bitter. “Have fun.”

“Well, I guess you could join us.”

“No, no, you have fun with the kids. This will give me time to look for a place.”

“You’re moving out?”

Another knock on my door. I looked up, as if someone was going to open it, but remembered it was locked. After tossing the journal on the bed, I walked toward the door, finally ready to tell everyone to leave. I wasn’t ready to face them, but I was ready for them to be gone so I could crack open a bottle without judgement. Something stopped me as I took my first step. A dark blue journal stuck out like a sore thumb in that box. I stepped back, not fully focussed on the conversation. My hand grasped hold of it before I immediately let it go.

"You said you wanted a divorce; I'm just giving you what you want. I'm not one of those women who's going to keep the house and kick you out."

"Well, if that's what you want," Nate said. His voice was strained. I frowned.

"What ***I*** want?"

"Yeah, if you want to move out, I'll do what I can to help."

"Oh, how generous of you. To want to help your pitiful wife."

"That's not what I said."

"You didn't have to." I snorted and rolled my eyes. I tapped my foot.

"Okay, I'll take the hint. Let you know when we're on our way tomorrow."

He hung up before I could retort the sharp response hanging on my tongue.

"Nevaeh, we're leaving. You obviously have some shit to work out," Mark said before he stomped away. I could imagine his head shaking as he walked away. I counted to sixty, heard the door click. Pretended I could hear their footsteps as they shuffled away before I walked out of my room. I stuck my head out first to make sure no one assaulted me. When I was sure no one was in my house anymore, I walked down my hall. Straight to the cabinet in the kitchen with varying alcohol. No wine tonight. My hand grasped a bottle of whiskey. The good stuff.

I popped the cork off and took a long swig. I ignored the burn as I took a couple of gulps. Something felt off. Something felt wrong. I pulled the bottle away from my lips and whipped my mouth. The image of the blue journal shot across my mind. As if in a panic, I ran back to my room. The bottle sloshed as I ran. I didn't care. Something was wrong. Adrenaline pushed through my stomach, and I gasped, choking on my breathing, trying to get back control of my body as it pushed me forward.

I made it back to my room quicker than should have been possible. Fear was choking me. Fear was filling every empty part of me. The realization of how alone I was, hitting every painful nerve.

I grabbed that blue journal and flipped it open. The pages fluttered to the middle of it. My father's handwriting.

Oh God! I'm screaming! For my daughter. For my wife. For my children. Why do you take? Why do we have to lose those closest to us? I hate you for this! For taking me from my family! I hate you for taking my son. I hate you for putting the burden on Nevaeh. Why does death always win?

My shoulders slumped forward, and my hand went to my mouth. It shook as I covered it. I could feel the desperation in my father's words. I could hear his voice. He lashed out, uncharacteristically, of who I knew. My father had always shown an attitude of unyielding faith. He guided our family with a secure mind, wrapped in the armor of God. He was never harsh, abusive, or rude. He was always kind, but firm.

I looked further, wondering if it would continue. Hoped it would. The relief that my father wasn't perfect was a soothing balm across my aching heart.

The writing changed.

CHAPTER NINE

Alone

It wasn't my father's writing anymore. A part of me knew that. There was a wave of irritation at the revelation. I didn't want to see someone else's writing. I wanted to see my daddy's. I read anyway, and wrinkled my nose in disgust at what I read.

Just another fake ploy of God talking, just like my mom bragged about. So much for relating to daddy.

You will be still and listen. MY grace is unyielding. My glory unending. Death is but a crumbling pillar. Death is a necessity where lessons must be learned! There is no power over the blessing of grace that I give. Death cannot win. I have already won. Do not fear, do not doubt my power. Do not doubt my plan! For I am always with you!

I slammed the book shut and tossed it on the bed. I shook my head. What should I have expected? My phone vibrated, and I looked down to see that it was a text from my mother. *I love you so much Nevaeh. You are going to do amazing things when you decide to let people see through your cracks.*

I frowned. Despite my mother and I never being close, which made my father's passing so much harder, she knew me so well. She saw through every social media post. She spoke up and confronted me with every act of inspiration I didn't have the strength to follow through on. What was the word? If you can't take it, don't dish it? Or the other one she frequently used; I heard her voice in the back of my mind. “Nevaeh, you need to learn to take a dose of your own medicine. If you can post about it, then you can live it. You have more power than you realize.”

Destined for greatness. I snorted. Yeah, destined to feel good by the comments other people posted. The comments of praise I would throw in her face. How I changed their lives, how they confronted their husbands. There were negative comments as well, but rarely. It gave me a high that alcohol couldn’t. I looked at my phone. The icon for YouTube, TikTok, Instagram, and even Snap Chat with the red numbered notifications. I grinned halfheartedly. I’ll bet it didn’t reach my eyes, if anyone had bothered to stay.

Why, when I was a social media icon, did I feel so alone? I didn’t stew on that thought for too long. I had lots of friends. Nate and I always had a party. We always had people over. Where was everyone, though? I didn’t really hear from anyone except Sky. But even she had recently distanced herself except for our occasional Chai Addicts moments when she needed content. Everyone came around when they needed or wanted something. What about me? Alcohol. That's what I wanted. That burn tickling my tongue as it lit a fire down my throat and warmed my belly. When social media didn't fill the void, alcohol always did. Ah! That's what I was doing. At some point, I didn't even remember, but I had lightly balanced the bottle on the carpet. The cork was probably still on the counter where I'd popped it off and tossed it in desperation. I grasped hold of it and smiled. I wasn't alone. I had my daddy's journals and a bottle of whisky. A perfect combination.

I pushed up from the carpet and grabbed another journal. This one was a dark brown. It was faded, the pages swollen. I flipped it open, and a daisy fell out. A large fat daisy. The sweet scent lifted into my nose. A subtle smell, the coming of spring.

Images filled my mind of being outside playing. The fat cheeks of my sister, when she was very young, excited to give Daddy that daisy. He'd kept it. In fact, as I looked, tears again filled my eyes. I must have an attached water jug to my eyeballs because those tears just kept coming. My cheeks were puffy and raw. I kept swiping at them, but they flowed harder as I realized the swollen pages were from all the flowers Rebekah had given him through the years, not from the ink on the page.

The pages were full of his writing, not as expressive as mine, but full of prayers and a simplicity of the days. Important days filled those pages, and prayers over my sister. I sucked in a breath; longing filled my body.

"Oh, Daddy. Why did you have so much faith in someone who took you, anyway?"

Death has a purpose when there are lessons to be learned. The words spun through my head quickly and disappeared. I shook my head. Nope. No reason. There was no justifiable reason for my brother dying. There was no justifiable reason for my daddy giving everything to his powerful God, only to receive nothing in return.

A buzzing burst through my veins as I took another long gulp. I whirled the bottle around and found that Rebekah's journal was still sitting on my lap. A small bit of liquid popped out and dropped into the open journal as I swirled it. Some words smudged as the amber liquid was sucked into the page. I glared at it, then looked closely at the bottle. It was almost gone. How full was it when I grabbed it? Had I already drunk half of it?

I knew I had one gulp left before all the pain would dissipate and I could escape the confines of my mind's prison. Then the creativity would hit. Most people who got drunk got stupid or angry. I got happy and creative. In the next couple of hours, I would post several times about divorce and healing. I would post about losing a loved one. I was already planning what I would say in my posts. I giggled. Tonight, I wasn't going to wallow in self-pity anymore. I was going to get back at Nate for being a jerk. For every husband I had, and their own stupidity in losing me.

I swigged the last gulp and tossed the bottle down. It rolled away from me and sat there winking on that stupid carpet. Back to square one, I imagined it bursting. The shards of glass would fly across the carpet. A piece of glass would be hidden in the carpet after I cleaned it up, only for me to step on it barefoot weeks from now. It would hurt, but it would be a refreshing pain.

To my disappointment, nothing happened. Instead, I lost myself in a drunken stupor. I had a sexy picture of myself posted and a long description of what crappy people my ex-husbands were without mentioning names. It was all hearsay about taking your power back as a woman, but everyone who knew me closely would know who I was talking about. I didn't care. I posted it anyway.

Betrayal can leave bitter wounds. Infected, nasty, and festering. I guess something finally burst out in me. I'm sure I would regret it tomorrow when I was nursing another hangover and I dealt with the repercussions from Nate, but for now, it didn't matter. Nothing did. I waited, stared at my phone expectedly. Come on! Where are the comments? For the first time in months, my post didn't blow up. I swear I heard crickets.

Then I heard a knock on my door. Who the heck?

I walked drunkenly to my bedroom door, the bottle catching my eye. “What’re you uh.. lookin at?” I huffed out while I stuck my tongue out at it. I stooped down and picked it up before stomping down my hallway as someone banged on the door again. I tossed the bottle in the trashcan as I stumbled past and threw the door open.

“Oh thank goodness, you’re still awake,” Sky said.

I felt my eyes bulge, trying to remember what she was supposed to be doing. Something about popcorn and a movie with her kids.

“What you doin here?” I asked.

She looked at me, her red curly hair pinned in a messy bun. Her green eyes squinted. She sniffed me and I moved away. The gesture reminded me of my mom.

“You’re drunk?”

“That uh.. depends. Whose askin?” I swayed and giggled as I put my hand over my mouth.

Sky rolled her eyes and shook her head. She had a bag in one hand, and her other hand rested on her full hips. She was shorter than me and her figure curvier. I always hated her for it. In the same way, she hated me for how slim I was. We used to compare ourselves in the mirror. She would grab her belly rolls and make them talk, while I poked my hip bones in disgust.

"Nevaeh, you need to get your shit together."

"Scuse me?"

She rolled her head and her neck popped. The noise made me nauseous. Uh. Maybe I drank too much this time. She pointed to her chest before she jabbed her finger into mine with each word she uttered. "You are talking to an ex-alcoholic, remember? You have a problem. You might not know it, but you have a problem. Your mom called me because she was worried. Said to tell you she loves you."

I laughed. It reminded me of yesterday and my manic laugh. Sky stood stoic; she was used to my outbursts.

"Yeah, yeah, so funny. Here. Drink this," she said as she pulled out a large bottle of body armor. I looked at it and gagged.

"Oh, good lord woman. You're a hot mess tonight, huh? Was Malachi that bad?"

Ah, so my mom told her everything. More pity. Great. A roll of nausea burst through my body. I gagged again.

"The bathroom is that way," Sky said as she pointed down the hall toward my bedroom. I spun on my heal and took off for the bathroom. I heard her footsteps as I made it just in time and held onto the toilette. "Praying to the porcelain Gods," Mark used to joke. Mark. My peace keeping addict brother.

"What's all this?" Sky asked from my bedroom as I continued to hurl. I heard her quick intake of breath as I'm sure she opened a journal. Damn it to hell Nevey, you forgot to put them all away.

"Nothing, Sky. Just stupid God talk," I gasped out as another wave of retching overtook my body.

"Well, maybe you should start listening," she said. Her voice was low and laced with something I couldn't place.

I wiped my mouth and flushed the toilette. I put my head against it. The cool porcelain was helping to chase away the spinning and heat that had spread across my body. "You're one to talk. You don't believe in God. You're a pagan. You believe we are as we are." I'm surprised I could get the words out clearly without slurring. Especially considering the bathroom looked like it was on a slow merry go round.

"Actually, I believe in God. If I didn't, I wouldn't have gotten away from my addiction. I believed that, but I haven't for a long time now. I just don't bring it up to you because you won't listen anyway. You're so stubborn and self-absorbed that you won't listen to anyone."

"I am not," I shot out. I could feel the drunken stupor beginning to burn away like the buzz had earlier. No, don't leave me with her.

"Nevey, I love you to death, and we used to love getting drunk together, but we're not teenagers anymore. It's time to grow up. Didn't you wonder why I've been so distant?"

"Yeah, and I hate you for it."

I heard her sigh. When I finally pushed up from the toilette and walked out of my bathroom, she had a hand bent behind her back. It tugged on a loose strand of hair that hung at the back of her neck. It was a nervous tick. She stared at the box and the journals I still had laying outside of it. She tilted her head to the side, and I followed her gaze to the blue one. The bag was still draped in her hand.

"So, you gonna leave me too?" I whined.

"Oh, Nevey." She sounded exhausted. "Who cares if I leave you? Who cares if everyone leaves you?"

"I do," my voice was a whisper.

"Well, you shouldn't. Not when you have someone who will never leave you."

"Whose that? Nate? He wants a divorce, so you're wrong there."

"No, I mean God. Nate messaged me, so I know."

"He messaged you?"

"Well yeah, he was worried, and shocked you didn't care."

"I've been through four divorces, Sky. I know how it goes down."

"Oh, aren't you so smart?" She wrinkled her nose. Her lip curled as she looked me up and down. I looked down at myself. I had vomit on my shirt, and I didn't even notice. Gross.

"Here's what we're gonna do, Nevey. I'm a mom, so I earned the right to do this. You're gonna get your shit together starting right now."

"There's nothing wrong with me."

"Hmm, do you go straight for a bottle when you're overwhelmed?" She raised an eyebrow. I looked away and crossed my arms. "That's what I thought."

I glared at her as I yanked my shirt off and stomped toward Nate's dresser. Screw his divorce, I needed his scent on me. I grabbed his shirt and threw it over me before I unhooked my bra and yanked it out of the armhole.

"You know Nate swears you don't love him? That you haven't for a while? That all you care about is social media."

"Oh bull, I'm always doing shit for him. You know this is the first day I've really had without the kids in months? Does he help me clean? No. Who takes care of the kids twenty-four seven? I'll tell you who. me. On top of trying to keep up on bringing extra money in so he doesn't have to stress. As far as I'm concerned, a little drinking is my reward."

"Well, he doesn't see it that way."

"Well, he can suck on my right toe."

"You know, some people are into that kind of thing. You never know."

I pursed my lip at the failed attempt to lighten the mood. She rolled her eyes. "You are as stubborn as Daddy."

My heart lurched, and the room spun as her hand flitted out to stroke the blue leather journal. She'd always called my father Daddy, ever since hers left when she was seven.

“What is it about these journals that seems familiar?”

CHAPTER TEN

Unending grace

I looked at the journals and chewed on my lip. I'd noticed it too. A realization made my eyes widen. I stepped forward and flipped the box over, started grabbing journals and looking more closely at them. Two had Mark's name stamped across the leather. Two had Rebekah's, and two had Malachi's. One was only a few pages, but it had Mathew's name stamped on the front. The rest of the journals had my name.

A vague memory of my father sitting down in his study, writing. The whispers of his voice as he wrote. I always just thought he was praying. But I realized there were eighteen journals. Ten of them had my name on them. One was full of prayers and stamped on the front was God in all caps. The rest were simple details of my siblings. Matthew's was the one that hurt the most. When I flipped it open, a flat rock fell out. The word Love written on it in sharpie. The journal was only a few pages and full of pain and desperation that he'd drowned. That I'd killed him.

"Nevey? Is everything ok?"

I'd forgotten Sky was there. I looked at her and bit my lip. "They're familiar, because we used to run past Daddy's study as he was writing in them."

"What do you mean?"

"Remember, we used to ask him to play when my mom was at work? He would always say, after I'm finished? We would both curiously look over his shoulder and he would snap the journal shut. I didn't notice… I didn't realize…"

"But the things he wrote in weren't labeled."

"Yeah, but they were there. He always had this blue one on his bedside table, remember? It just had a lock glued to it."

I looked closer at it to make sure I was right. Sure enough, there was a scuff on both sides where a leather strip had ripped off.

"If that's true, then why aren't there more? Why are there only two for them, and the rest in your name? Why didn't your mom just give you the ones with your name on it?"

"I don't think she did anything besides open the box and see my name was on a journal, Sky. I don't think she knew."

"Well, that's weird."

"Yeah, I don't get it either. Wanna read them with me?"

"Umm… well, I know you don't want to face the simple fact, Nevey… but we need to talk…"

"I promise, I will start working on myself.. but right now, this feels really important."

She looked back at the stack I'd dumped out. Her gaze drifted to the discarded box. "Alright. But we are having the other conversations," she said as she pulled out a thermos.

"Chai latte?"

She beamed at me and winked. "Not just a chai latte, a warm latte with Carmel and…," she pulled out a bottle, "whip cream!" She popped off the top and squirted a foamy line into her mouth.

I couldn't help but laugh.

"See! This is so much better than bitter alcohol," she said through the mouthful of whip cream.

I wasn't about to agree with her, so I shrugged and grabbed the can from her.

"Hey," she exclaimed as I squirted it into my own mouth.

I grinned, my cheeks puffed out and my eyes squinted. "I guess it's alright."

"It always made me feel cheap. It didn't matter how expensive it was." She frowned as she popped the thermos open. She sniffed it and sighed before she plopped down onto the carpet. I looked down at her and shook my head. She studied the thermos, oblivious to my staring.

She took a gulp and closed her eyes. Her lips smacked together, and I shivered at the sound. Gross. I hated the sound of lip smacking. She finally looked up at me while she still held it to her lips. “What? We gonna do this or not?” she asked as she tilted her head to the side.

I huffed out a breath, looked at the journals, and plopped down beside her. She pulled out a king-size KitKat bar, our favorite, along with a bag of popcorn.

“Good lord woman, it’s like you came prepared for me to be starting my period,” I said as I chuckled.

“It was meant to be a peace offering, but I guess now it’s for entertainment.” She shoved the thermos into my hand. I took it and squirted another mouthful of whip cream before I handed the can back to her.

“So where are we starting, and what are we looking for?”

"I don't know Sky, the answers to life?"

"Well, then we're gonna be here for a while."

I took a gulp of the chai latte; the sweet nectar and spices licked my tongue. Yummy. OK, maybe she's right. This drink could beat even the best tasting alcohol. I chose not to respond to her as she peeled open the KitKat bar. She broke it and handed a piece to me. I took it gladly and realized I hadn't really eaten. I took a bite and grabbed the blue journal again. This time I wanted to start at the beginning.

"Oh, you got the good one. Alright then, I'm gonna read this one." She held up a light red notebook, smaller than the rest. It was more faded and looked older. It had Malachi's name on it. I raised my eyebrows and shrugged before I focused back on the first page of the dark blue leather journal that was labeled to God. My daddy's handwriting scrolled across the page, only a couple of simple sentences. Something I'd been asking for my entire life. With each divorce. With each unpleasant situation.

God, I come to you in confidence, in question. Why did you put it on our hearts to use Heaven? To name Nevaeh? Did we curse her?

I read further, absorbed in the page now. Sucked in the information. I was so focused that I didn't hear my front door opening. I didn't realize Sky got up and took the journal with her.

You are my child. All who I call to be my children will be called by name. I speak life into your name. Do you doubt your name? Do you doubt your purpose? I spoke life into her name, as I spoke life into yours. A curse is of negative bearing. I am grace. I am love. My grace is unending. My love is all-consuming.

I spoke life into her name, to bear witness to my power. To be led beyond a measure of your beliefs, a beacon of healing and submission to my love. She will experience a pain not measurable. As you discipline your child, is it not painful? Discipline is a necessity as the air I fill your lungs with. Do not be afraid! With discipline comes the knowledge of responsibility. Your heart is heavy, cast your burden on me! I am with her always!

I read it several times, trying to make sense of it. My daddy. He seemed so weak to me now. Putting his faith in something that would cause his youngest daughter so much pain. How could he talk to someone who openly said it would put me in more pain than could be measured? Who does that? Insane people. Expecting a different outcome, a different answer if they just keep doing it again or asking it over.

"Hey, Nevey?"

"Huh?" I was still focused on the words.

"Mama!" the small voices filled my heart with joy as a smile spread across my lips.

"Oh, my babies," I exclaimed. I dropped the journal in my lap and threw my arms open as the small footsteps pattered toward me. What time was it?

"Well, hello my little munchkins," I said as they jumped into my arms. Laughter filled my lungs as they tipped me backwards for a second before I got control of the momentum. They shoved on their tippy toes to knock me over. Their giggles were a soothing balm to my soul. I had my eyes clamped shut and held them close. My face rested against our son's shoulder.

"Nevey, can we talk?" Nate's voice was quiet. I sucked my lip into my mouth. Keep it together, Nevey, no more crying today.

"Isn't it time for bed?" I asked as they finally pulled back.

"We wanna play!" our daughter said as she jumped up and down on the balls of her feet.

I smiled, and a giggle bubbled up through my chest.

My gaze slid to Nate. He stood just in front of our bedroom doorway. My eyebrows rose because his eyes were swollen and red.

CHAPTER ELEVEN

Lost

I rang my hands and pulled our two children closer to me. Sky stood behind him as he ran a hand through his hair. His eyes were wide.

"No one called you?" he asked.

"Okay kiddos, let's give Mommy and Daddy some privacy. Let's go get ready for bed with aunty Sky," Sky said with a large smile plastered on her face.

The protests and stomping feet made me laugh. "Go on you two, you know you better listen to aunty Sky, or she will get you. Mommy and Daddy won't save you either."

Sky gave a warning growl, and the kids ran out of our room screaming as she stomped after them. Nate shut the door quietly, but I could still hear Sky as she screamed that the tickle monster was coming. I continued to grin and turned my attention to Nate.

He was standing with his back to me, his forehead flush against the door. Sobs wracked his body. I looked down at my hands. There was melted chocolate where I'd forgotten I was holding the rest of the KitKat bar. I looked back at Nate, who had slid down to his knees and was now slumped over.

I shot up like a canon and warning bells sounded in my head. "Nate? Nate what's wrong?"

He continued to sob.

I dropped the remainder of the chocolate bar, not caring that it would be a pain to clean up later and wiped the melted goo on my pants. I sped up to him and knelt down beside him. I reached out a hand, but then pulled it away. Divorce. He wanted a divorce. I'm not allowed to touch him, he's not mine anymore. "Nate? Talk to me. It's okay, whatever it is, I'm sure we can get through it. It's not a big deal. I respect your decision for a divorce."

He sobbed harder. Again, I stretched out my hand and pulled it away. Our knees were touching, both of us faced the closed door. You could still hear Sky's muffled cries of delight. I turned my body to bend slightly forward so I could try and see his face.

When his face turned toward mine slightly, and tears silently slid down his cheeks, I jerked back. His expression was full of misery.

"What is it?" I whispered.

He shuddered.

"Nate, what is it?"

He looked away. I could barely hear his voice. I thought I heard him wrong. "Your mom, a drunk driver hit her," his voice broke. I took a deep breath, his throat cleared, and his voice shuddered out, "Nevey, she was dead on impact."

I reared back. A roaring filled my ears. I plopped on my butt and scrambled away as he reached for me. “You’re, you’re lying!” I didn’t mean to raise my voice, but I couldn’t help it. My chest clinched. My breathing came out in brief gasps.

“Baby girl, I’m so, so, sorry. I thought someone would have told you…” He reached for me again and I jerked away.

“It can’t be true… she just told Sky how much she loves me. She just messaged me. She can’t be. I saw her. You’re lying.”

“Nevey, she was driving…”

“No…no…No!” I wailed.

Nate didn’t lie to me. He always felt honesty was the best policy.

“Yes Nevey. I am so sorry…”

I sat there rocking, and Nate moved forward and pulled me to him. Tears didn’t come. They didn’t when Daddy took his last breath either. I think something snapped in me when I realized my brother had died in that pool. I remember the screams that came out of my mouth. My mother’s wails long after everyone had given up on CPR. How despite my mom's pain, she'd picked herself up, dusted herself off, knelt, and prayed.

"He took her. He's going to take everyone," I shuddered.

"Took who, Nevey? Who took who?"

I continued to rock. Nate rocked with me as I mumbled to myself. The mad hatter came to mind. The stupid word Blue journal kept flashing in my head. I repeated it over and over as I screamed at myself that I didn't want to read the journals anymore. I screamed into Nate's chest, and he gripped me as I rocked.

"Breathe Nevey, just breathe."

I held my breath. Everything was too painful. I didn't want to feel the air scraping against my chest. I jerked involuntarily; my body wanted oxygen. I didn't want it; I should be the one dead. Not Mama and Daddy.

"Breathe, Nevey," Nate's firm voice laced around me like a comforting blanket. I was numb while also in excruciating pain. Maybe if she hadn't spent so much time here, cleaning for me. Waiting for me to come out of my room.

"I can't. I can't. It hurts, everything hurts," I gasped out.

"I know baby, I know. I'm so sorry. Come on, slow breaths, one, two, three… ok breath in…"

He counted slowly with every breath in and every breath out. Pausing between, and rocking with me. Ignoring my mumbles to myself. I clung to his shirt.

"Why does everyone leave me? Why does everyone get taken?" I asked to myself.

"I'm not going anywhere, Nevey."

I choked on a brewing sob. "But you want a divorce."

"Now is not the time, Nevey."

I choked out a breath and continued silently crying. My body and mind felt empty. My soul broken. Everything in me was completely raw. Too much Nevey, today was just too much. I felt Nate rise as my body slumped with apparent exhaustion. He laid me gently on the bed. Tired, I was so tired. My head sunk into the pillow. "No, I.. I can.. Sky, Sky." My words were a blurred mess.

"I'll tell her, Nevey."

He leaned over and kissed my forehead. My eyes fluttered shut. I could feel him pull the comforter up to my nose and I sank down further into our bed. I rolled over subconsciously as I heard the door creak open. I heard Sky as her knees hit the floor, her body falling against Nate's chest. I pulled his pillow closer to me and curled against it.

"You took everything from me. I will never forgive you for this," I hissed out. To whom? I wasn't sure.

I cringed at the sound of Sky's broken cry, half asleep, but I heard a voice in my head. It rang out with a force that even my tired body jolted at.

You may wander, you may become lost. But I will always find you.

CHAPTER TWELVE

Broken and damned

The next few days were quiet. I could feel Nate tiptoeing around me. I kept myself busy cleaning and cooking. I couldn't get myself to post anything. I didn't want the attention. It seemed so trivial that I'd ever wanted it. The eyes of other people, when I wasn't even paying attention to the eyes of the ones I was supposed to love.

Sky had messaged and called me several times, but I didn't respond. Shock and depression had a funny way of shutting a person down. I looked down into the large hazel eyes of Mysty, our six-year-old daughter and her four-year-old brother Merkal, who was her shadow. They looked at me innocently, each with a plate of food in front of them. Their eyes were identical to Nate's but filled with an innocence that adults tend to lose. I'd woken up at four and made miniature pancakes, homemade orange juice, eggs, bacon, sausage, and homemade biscuits and gravy with hash browns.

To an even bigger surprise of myself, I cleaned everything up before the kids even traipsed out from their rooms, complaining about being hungry. Their tummies grumbled in expectation of the food.

Merkal flicked his fork and pushed me out of my thoughts. Some of his food went flying. He giggled.

"Merkal Dorrance, not funny. You know better."

"Mama, he's just playing," Mysty said as her little arms crossed and her chin titled up in defense of her brother. With the way they'd been acting, I was sure that they knew something was wrong, even if they didn't understand it.

"Hey," Nate said as he walked into the kitchen.

I'd been sleeping in bed with the kids. I was switching back and forth between their rooms, squeezing into their twin sized beds every night. I hadn't bothered to wake Nate up. If he wanted a divorce, he needed to learn how to wake up by himself.

"Good morning," I said. I sipped on my large cup of coffee.

"How are you?"

"Can we skip the niceties? Your breakfast is in the oven," I said.

Mysty and Merkal stared at me with wide eyes. I pushed a smile onto my face and winked. "Mama is gonna get dressed, you two eat your food, okay?"

"Were not hungry," Mysty said defiantly and Merkal nodded in agreement while he shoved his plate away.

"Listen to your mother or we're gonna have a problem," Nate said.

I didn't want to feel anything, but my heart felt as if someone had squeezed it uncomfortably.

"Do you both understand? Your mama worked really hard to make this breakfast. You're both gonna eat it."

I looked at him and his gaze softened. He reached his hand up as if he would fold a stray hair behind my ear but changed his mind. His hand drifted slowly back to his side, and he looked back at his coffee. I spun on my heel and walked away.

When I got to our room, my gaze traveled to the box of my father's journals. I'd woken up the morning after I fell apart to them placed neatly back in the box beside the bed. My lips pursed and I glared at them. Maybe I would burn them. I stomped over and scooped up the box. I shoved it into our closet before I began picking out clothes to wear for the day.

~ ~ ~

"I'm leaving Nevey. There's an issue at the store."

I'd locked myself in the bathroom, but I still heard his muffled voice through the door.

"Alright."

"Kids are in their rooms getting dressed." I heard his breathing as he waited for a response. I couldn't come up with anything as I opened my mouth and closed it. The door flexed as he pushed his head against it. I made a noise like I was busy.

Just leave, I can't take this hot and cold.

"I love you Nevaeh," he breathed.

I put my hands up to my throat and looked up at the ceiling. I didn't say anything out loud, instead I mouthed that I loved him too. More than he would ever know. I was just too hard to love. Too hard to handle. I pulled my phone from my pocket to distract myself. There were several notifications, but seeing all the people I didn't know, their likes and comments, when my family hadn't even contacted me, made me angry.

I wanted to disappear, as if I'd never existed. I wondered if I could? Just disappear. Why not? A small smile flitted across my lips. Something tugged at my heart. Delete it all, Nevaeh. All of it. Who cares anymore?

Without second guessing myself, I clicked through every icon and went through deleting them. Each one with a thirty day hold in case I changed my mind. There goes two thousand or more, a month extra.

It was invigorating to remove every bit of who I had been pretending to be. To shut all my emotions down and just not care anymore.

"Mama?" Mysty's little voice said through the door.

I didn't realize I was crying till she slowly twisted the doorknob. I choked on a sob.

"Mama? You okay? Merkal has his pants on backwards and he won't listen to me."

I couldn't help but laugh as Merkal came stomping into the bathroom with his hands on his hips. I fell to my knees. Too much. It was all too much. I cried harder.

"Go, just get out. Mama needs a minute," I forced out.

Merkal's lip quivered as he stared at me in obvious offense.

"Oh, Mama… it's okay," Mysty said, and the sobs shook my body. Without hesitation, her eyes widened, and she walked up to me

quickly. She wrapped her arms around me and pulled me against her small chest. She played with my hair as my heart opened and shattered apart in a display of slivered glass. "It's okay Mommy, it's okay to cry. Sometimes we just gotta cry. You'll be okay."
We stayed like that; Mysty played with my hair to calm me down. My six-year-old daughter, taking responsibility for her broken mother as her brother leaned against the door frame with his pants on backwards. I finally pulled back. It wasn't getting better. I knew I was getting ready to fall apart.

"Are you okay now, Mommy?"

I wiped my eyes, my voice broke as I responded, "Yeah baby, Mommy loves you both so much. Thank you so much for taking care of Mommy. Why doesn't Mama put on a show and you guys can watch it in the playroom?"

"Yeah," they both shouted together.

"Whose gonna win to the playroom?" I asked. I hid my pain with a smile. Their small feet took off running as they shouted at each other who was going to win first.

~ ~ ~

I lasted for ten minutes. I stitched myself together, put on a brave face, got them drinks and snacks, and put on a movie before my body started to shake. “Alright babies, you have fun, Mama’s gonna shut the door so you have some nice and quiet you time.”

They didn’t respond, already focused on the movie. I tried to smile, but I had nothing left. I was empty. I tried to walk slowly from the room and shut the door lightly. I needed to get a job. How else was I going to support myself and two kids on my own? I walked to our liquor cabinet in the kitchen. I threw it open; desperation soaked my body in an attempt to numb the pain. Sky’s words echoed in my mind as I stared at the ten or more bottles in the cabinet. They got blurry. As if my hands weren’t my own, I grabbed them. One by one. Before I could change my mind, I dumped them into the sink.

“Is this what you want?” I threw my hands up, the last two bottles grasped in each one toward the ceiling before I poured them from above my head in the sink. “There you go. Happy? I have nothing left! What now?”

I fell to my knees, the bottles now sitting idle and empty on the counter. My knees hit the floor hard, as the floodgates from my tears burst open. I screamed, and curled into myself. “Why? Why do you do nothing but take? This is your fault. She believed in you, and you took her. You took everything from me. I have nothing to live for.”

I thought about the firearm Nate had gotten me for our anniversary the year before. For my safety, he had said as we went to the range and taught me how to use it. It would be so easy. Just wait for the kids to fall asleep for their nap, message Nate I needed him home and go in the car. It sounded like a relief. To end it all.

I didn’t want to fight anymore. I formulated a plan as I curled into a ball, shaking, and falling apart. Every piece of me felt like it was lying there. I grasped at the floor as if I could pick the pieces up. There was nothing to grab. When I'd decided that was the best plan, and that everyone would be better off without me anyways, my phone vibrated. I pulled it from my pocket. It was my Rebekah.

I know you're probably in a drunk stupor, nursing your pain away, but we're all scared and hurting. Mom went to get milk for French toast in the morning and a drunk driver hit her. That's what happened. I know you don't believe in God, and right now I really don't either, but this song made me think of you. Please listen to it. I love you always, little sis.

At the end of the message was a link to her Spotify and the song "*You say*" by Lauren Daigle. I frowned and clicked on the link. Well, I could at least give her stupid song a listen before I made myself disappear.

The music sent a fresh wave of sobs through my body as something bloomed inside of me. I felt every word on a cellular level that I never had before. I remembered hearing the song in my sister's car at some point, but this time, it rolled through me like a battering ram.

The song made me feel like it was talking to me. She knew me so well, even considering we weren't close. I stayed on my knees and listened carefully. As if my body had a mind of its own, I clasped my hands together, and for the first time in a long time I prayed. I prayed silently as the tears continued to roll down my cheeks.

Five minutes prior, I'd been contemplating my death. Now I was praying, my heart screaming out for someone I didn't even believe in. Begging for him to take it away, to just take everything. Nate wasn't a believer. Sky believed in something that was a higher power, but it wasn't God. Our other friends, the ones I knew would no longer be my friends once divorce number five was finished, they didn't believe in God either.

Why I felt the need to beg and grovel, I don't know, but the words that sliced through my mind next weren't my own. They were words that made me question my beliefs.

Or lack of.

CHAPTER THIRTEEN

Found

"L*ove has no bounds. I am love. Give me your burdens, cast your lost soul on me. I have found you! I will not forsake you, instead I have plans of grace. I have plans of love for you. Submit to me, for I am always with you!"*

Submit? What was I, a slave? Something inside told me it was my pride. The realization hit me that I was all alone and had been for a while. In crowded rooms, alone. On social media, alone. I didn't want to let go of my independence. That felt sexist and old school. I rang my hands together.

"Lay your burdens on me. Submit and know that I am God! Let go, my child, you have

fought long enough. I will fill your emptiness. Let your weary soul rest."

I held on tighter, terrified of what might happen if I didn't. I clung to that lifeline of pain and trauma.

"You will submit. Rejoice, child, and repent. Acknowledge me. I am love and lessons must be learned. When you discipline your children, does it make them laugh or does it cause discomfort? I will use you for great things. The enemy is powerful, but you, beside me, are stronger."

My shoulders hunched into each other. My sobs had slowed. I didn't want to submit to anyone, to be controlled by anyone. Never again.

"Submission isn't control, my child. Submission is allowing me to fill your empty and wandering heart."

I heard the coo bells going off. I could imagine Nate taking the kids from me as I blubbered about hearing from God. Thank that same God he was at work. Whack job, Nevey. I could hear it now. Why else would I be hearing voices in my head as I sobbed in a heap?

"I have seen you. I have seen your pain. Your struggle beyond measure. Seek your answers in the journals."

Honestly, Nevey, what else do you have to lose? Mama is gone. Daddy is gone. Nate is leaving you. What else really do you have to lose?

"Okay, Mr. all powerful, let's see what you offer," my voice was laced with contempt. I could imagine if this so called father was standing in front of me, he would roll his eyes and smack me across the face. I felt a warm weight drifting through my body. My breath hitched and, for the first time, I sucked in the air as if I'd been holding my breath for years. It filled my lungs, and a temporary spritz of freedom spread across my broken and wounded soul.

I took another grateful breath and pushed up from the floor. I padded to the kids' playroom and checked on them. They were both sprawled out on their miniature couch and in a deep sleep. My eyebrows rose and I looked at my watch. It was barely ten thirty. Oh, you're really determined huh? I imagined a chuckle drifting through the room on the still air.

My little pony played on the small flat screen Nate had hung on one of the walls. Apparently Mysty decided the other movie wasn't good enough. I couldn't help myself when a small smile spread across my lips. My heart swelled with love at the look of their peaceful cherub faces. So identical to the handsome while soft features of their daddy. I walked up to them both and ran my fingers through their hair.

"A taste of the love I have, for you. For all."

"Can you get out of my head? For years you were completely silent, now you won't shut up?" I whispered while I looked around the room, as if someone stood there, hidden in the thin air. Someone was going to diagnose me with multiple personality disorder or schizophrenia or something of the sort if they heard me. I snorted. Mysty groaned and re-situated herself.

Good going Nevey, you're gonna wake up the little innocent hellions. I stepped back slowly and quietly. Quickly I spun and tip-toed out the door. It probably looked quite comical the way I hopped from foot to foot. I swung the door shut, just a crack, enough to hear them when they woke up.

"I need to be a better mom," I said to the empty hall. I stood there holding the door knob. Images of me yelling, distracted by my phone, shooing them away when I did videos, self-absorbed in social media. Images of their little bodies, growing so quickly. It hurt. It seemed like every part of me felt empty. I never liked talking to my mom, because she always shoved God in my face, but in that moment, she was the one person I wanted to cry with. I wanted her to pray over me, to tell me it would be okay. I wanted her to explain why I was hearing things, and why I couldn't get anything right. I wanted my mama. Above all, I wanted my children to know they could always come to their mama and I wouldn't judge them.

Right then, I vowed to myself. It was time for a change. I hadn't been living, I was just surviving. Looking for gratification from everyone else without seeing what was right in front of me. The blessing God had blessed me with.

I stopped.

It was as if my face smacked into a brick wall. I didn't believe in God. Why was I vowing to change because he'd blessed me? I was here, wasn't I? While everything else around me was crumbling, I was here. Ignoring and scheming to end my own life. To cause more loss. To cause those closest to me to lose, to suffer just like I had.

I looked around and my chest expanded. I tried to suck in air, but it swelled in short gasps. My house. The house I'd built with my husband. So many blessings. Images burst through my mind. Every blessing. Every hurt, followed by a blessing. If I didn't believe, then why did I feel a peace that clouded my body? To chase the darkness I'd been fighting for so long?

"A blanket of Grace."

I remembered all the years I'd gone to church. Images of the services and how my mom would dress us all up. A determined and pinched expression would stay molded on her face while she loaded a squirming Mark and me into the car. Rebekah, Matthew, and Malachi were old enough to drive, but not old enough to live on their own. I never remembered listening to the sermons. I liked the music, but I always felt unwelcome and awkward. It probably didn't help that Mark always teased me.

I blinked a few times. I'd made it to my room, stuck in my trance of memories. I flapped my fingers and stared around. The laundry was gone. I didn't realize Nate had done it.

I walked to the closet. All my clothes were neatly hung up, even those that I didn't hang up were put away. *Oh, Nevey. You've been chasing others' approval for too long.*

Determination coursed through me, and I nodded to myself. I pulled the box from the corner of the closet I'd stuffed it in, originally prepared to burn all those journals.

Something in my heart pinged painfully. I rubbed my chest. Mama, I miss you so much. How am I supposed to do this without you?

I pulled out that dark blue journal first. An iron- clad determination and calm spread through my body. A blanket of grace, the voice had said? I didn't want to read Daddy's prayers for me and his other children. I wanted answers.

The second page was the one I flipped to.

CHAPTER FOURTEEN

Grace

What is life's worth if we do nothing but struggle? God, why is there so much pain? You found me. You healed me. You taught me how to cope without alcohol, but if I am going to die anyway, and if I have to go through all this pain, what's the point?

My mother just died. I had to watch her. What did her having Alzheimer's prove? Dad left you! I am still here, and still in pain!

I stopped reading. The pain in my chest was overwhelming. I remembered when Grandma had passed away. Papa had been beside himself. He turned completely away from God and blamed him. Disgusted because not only had he watched his wife of fifty years fall away from every part of what made her who she was, he had to watch her forget him before her body finally gave up. I shook my head. I tried to understand. Why did my Daddy have so much faith? Why did he keep writing to God?

If he was so powerful, why didn't he just wipe everything clean and start over? Why did he have to send his son as a sacrifice for us? Start it all over. Why hadn't he wiped Adam and Eve out so the rest of us didn't suffer?

I continued reading. This page was different. It was like my daddy was talking to God. He was journaling every feeling without a filter. I felt raw reading it, as if I was invading his privacy, but you can't invade the privacy of someone who is rotting bones and returning to dust.

God, I cry out to you! Why? I lost her! You took her from me. My father has fallen into the depths of a bottle. I loved my mom. I love my children. I love my wife. But Father, what is love? If you love us, why didn't you start over? End the suffering? You made a sacrifice, sending your son, yourself, to save us, but why not just start over?

I guess I thought more like my father than I expected. I nodded my head in agreement. His writing had stopped. The scrolled response was the same as every other page. Darker and more prominent. I'd never seen words come alive and take over a book. Not that I liked to read, but this, this was fascinating.

Sacrifice. Love is sacrifice. Love is faith. Love is grace.

I didn't understand. How did that make sense? Why did everything have to be so vague?

"For you wanting me to believe in you, you're not making it easy."

I turned the page, hoping for more, but the entire next three pages were the same exact words.

"Come on!"

"Mama?" a small voice broke through my quiet yell.

I cleared my throat before responding. “Hey bug, did you sleep well?”

Merkal rubbed his eyes. His hair was ruffled. He stepped toward me, and I wrapped my arms around him. “I love you, baby boy.”

“I’m not a baby,” he mumbled into my shoulder.

I chuckled and pulled back, feigning surprise. “You’re not? What do you mean?” I looked at him, pulled up his arm, dropped it and spun him around.

He giggled, and the sound warmed my heart. The distant pieces cracked.

“Mama, stop,” he gasped out, still giggling.

“Okay, okay, but only if you admit you’re Mama’s baby.”

“Fine, fine, I’m *your* baby. But I’m not a baby.”

“Okay, should we shake on it?”

He nodded his head firmly and stuck out his little hand. We shook and I winked at him.

“Mommy?” he asked as I pulled him onto my lap to turn the page.

“Hmm?”

"Is Grandma okay?"

The room grew silent. I could swear my heart stopped beating. How do you tell your four-year-old that Grandma isn't coming over for dinner anymore?

"Uh, well honey, Grandma had to go on a special adventure with God."

"Who is God?"

I bit my lips. The realization Nate and I hadn't really taught them about God. It made me nauseous, the idea of shoving something so trivial down my children's throats. Something so fake as un-ending grace and unconditional love. But something in me wanted him to know that love, even if it didn't exist for me, that it could exist for him and Mysty.

"God is the one who made you and me, baby. Remember Grandma always talked about him?"

"Well yeah, you said he's an old crack pot sitting in the sky telling people what to do." His frown in concentration of what I had indeed said made me chuckle.

"Yeah, Mama did say that. Maybe, Mama shouldn't have judged something she didn't really know or understand anything about?"

"You said it's mean to judge people and to make fun of them."

"Mama hasn't been very good on her word lately, huh?"

He shook his head and bit his lip. "I still love you, though. But you get angry and yell a lot. And you drink that really bitter stuff… that stuff that smells funny."

I sighed. Maybe we needed to go to church. I had so many questions, and how else was I going to find them out unless I started asking? I felt like something inside me was clicking into place.

"I'm sorry, honey. Mommy isn't gonna drink that stuff anymore. What do you think about going to church?"

He furrowed his brows and wrinkled his nose. "I don't wanna wear a stuffy suit. Grandma always makes me put a suit on."

"Well, honey, we're not gonna go to Grandma's church. We're gonna find our own… where you can play, and have fun, and learn how much God loves you."

His eyes widened, and his smile stretched across his face.

Oh boy. What did I just agree to?

CHAPTER FIFTEEN

Disbelief

"Come on babies, we're gonna be late. I have a good feeling about this one," I said while getting Mysty's jacket on. It'd been raining for two days now. The entire yard was flooded. It was a relief, and I loved the rain, but the kids were getting sour from being cooped up in the house.

"We're going to a new one? Do you think they'll have snacks?" Mysty said as she looked up at me.

"Ah, a woman after my own heart. I'm sure they will." I winked and kissed her on the forehead. She giggled.

"Mama, I don't wanna go to another old people's church."

"Merkal! It wasn't old people. It was just a small chapel, but I think I found one you guys will like."

"They better have snacks," Merkal huffed out and glared at me. "I don't think I like this church business."

Behind my hand, I hid a laugh. "I guess we will see after this one, okay?"

He pulled on his lip before he nodded firmly. We had went to church that same weekend, I told him we would. Mysty had been unsure and confused, but said she trusted me. So far we'd gone to five, and not found one that extended beyond one service. I'd talked to several pastors, looking for answers. It was the same every time. Automatic judgement for questioning, a lack of acceptance, and alienation.

"You're going to church again?" Nate asked as I grabbed the keys off the hook.

"Just looking for answers. I'm still trying to get a job so I can get out of the house for you."

"Nevey, I told you to take your time. It's not a race."

"Well, sleeping on a twin bed and awkwardly walking around the house isn't very comfortable."

I turned toward him. He sat at the bar top eating the breakfast I'd made for him and the kids. I was having a hard time eating. Instead, I busied myself by pouring over my daddy's journals every day, cleaned, and studied my Bible. I'd started praying too, silently, not sure what to say. I prayed for Nate, and his happiness. I wasn't sure who was listening because I couldn't seem to get my mouth to say words out loud. Hopefully whatever I was talking to could read minds. My mama and daddy always said God could see your mind and heart, and I finally hoped that was true.

Five weeks and my mother's funeral had come and gone. Malachi hadn't even shown up to the funeral. I texted him a long and disgusted message about it, but he never responded.

Rebekah and Mark, I finally got the nerve to speak to more. We spoke a little more than we had in years. When I explained to them what I was doing, the conversation was tense.

~ ~ ~

"I'm trying to figure it out, but there are things in those journals, things I did, that are talked about differently, that Daddy didn't know. I'm trying to get answers."

"That's cool, Nevey," Mark had said flatly.

I tilted my head to the side, looked between them. We were all sitting on my couch. I invited Mark and Rebekah after Sky informed me she needed a Chai Addicts night. We each held a steaming cup of chai latte. Yeah, alcohol wasn't so great when you had this to fill your belly.

Rebekah had snorted. "I'll believe that when I see it."

"Oh, come on guys, have a little more enthusiasm. Nevey has sacrificed a lot based on faith," Sky had said.

Sacrifice. Faith. Love.

"I wouldn't go that far," I retorted while I fiddled with a loose strand of hair.

"Nevey, you deleted all your social media. You could have been living on your own already… Oh shoot." She looked around with wide eyes. At that time, it'd been three weeks since Nate had told me he wanted a divorce.

"Living on your own? What's she talking about?" Mark asked.

I ignored him and studied my mug before I took a long gulp.

Sky looked at me and mouthed; "Sorry."

"I'm not forgiving you that easy," I mouthed back.

Her expression cringed. My head whipped around at the sound of Rebekah's voice. "Oh my God… you're getting a divorce."

Mark chuckled. "Yeah right, Nevey finally met her soul mate. Right? Fifth one's the charm."

Rebekah's eyes widened. "Holy crap… you're turning into the woman at the well."

"What?" I said, thankful for the change of subject. I didn't remember that story, although I hadn't gotten very far in my studying.
"Honestly. Haven't you learned anything? It's in John. Here, get your Bible."

My mouth popped open.

"What? You don't think I'm looking for answers too?" she asked.

"Someone wanna tell me what's going on?" I heard Mark ask as I walked into the entryway to get my bible from the table.

I walked back into the living room. Sky was whispering in his ear.

"Come on, Sky!"

"What? He deserves to know!"

"No one deserves to know my business."

"Oh, give me that thing," Rebekah said as she thrust out her hand.

"Nevey, I love you, but come on. Five guys? Is there gonna be a lucky number six?"

"No, Mark. If and when Nate and I decide to divorce, I am never marrying someone else again."

"Heard that before," Sky said under her breath.

"Oh, shut up all of you. Here it is. John 4: 1-42. Your translation is a little weird. Where did you get this Bible?"

"The Bible store. Daddy got it for me for my sixteenth birthday, remember? When I was really going to church," I said with wide eyes.

"Oh, I remember," Rebekah said, her nicely shaped eyebrow pushed up in annoyance.

"I remember, too. You were a massive dork. You used to take it to school, as well."

"Shut up Mark, I did not." I stuck my tongue out at him and pushed my mug up to my lips.

"No. I remember that you always had it pushed up against your chest," Sky said.

"That was Rebekah. I never got really into the Bible."

Every single one of them laughed.

"What?"

Rebekah snorted. She still held my Bible in her hand. The pages were bent and worn. I hadn't noticed. There were several places where tabs had been ripped off through the years.

"You were as bad as mother for about a year, till you met what's his name. Then it went all downhill from there and you started drinking and partying."

"Yeah, maybe it was all the drugs you did. I know I'm forgetful because of all the drugs I did," Mark said and winked before he hid behind his own mug. He smacked his lips together.

My body buzzed with frustration. I clinched my hands against the mug. I never did drugs. I just drank a lot. Mark was the addict. I squinted at him; my brows furrowed in concentration. I didn't remember any of that. I just remembered partying and having fun with Paul. He was my first marriage; it lasted six months.

"You know I left as soon as he tried to get me to try meth?"

Mark looked at me with a wounded expression.

"Okay, can you just explain why you're saying I'm the woman at the well?"

"About time. Anyways, even with your weird translation it will still get the point across,"

Rebekah said. She shimmied her butt to get comfortable while one hand, held the Bible open and one still held her mug. The mug my mom had gotten me for my twenty-first birthday. It was decorated with flowers, and the word grace was scrolled across the side in cursive. How fitting. That word was popping up everywhere.

Rebekah paused, I'm assuming for dramatic effect, cleared her throat and began reading. I squinted as she read. My mouth popped open. She looked at me sidelong before continuing. Everyone had gone quiet. I partially zoned out, till she got to verse fifteen.

~~~

"The woman said to Him, "Sir, give me this water, that I may not thirst, nor come here to draw."
Jesus said to her, "Go, call your husband, and come here."
The woman answered and said, "I have no husband."
Jesus said to her, "You have well said, 'I have no husband,' for you have had five husbands,
~~~

and the one whom you now have is not your husband; in that you spoke truly."

~~~

I shoved the mug back up to my lips and let it sit there. My gaze bounced around for several moments. "I'm sorry Beks, how does this make me the woman at the well? I have five husbands, but I'm still currently married."

"Oh, wise observation, miss visionary. You are currently married. But let's be honest, how long have you guys been having problems? Who called it this time? You? No, I bet it was him, huh?"

"Rebekah!" Sky said as she shot up from my couch.

"It's okay Sky, she's not wrong. It was that obvious?"

She nodded her head. "I don't even see you, but like twice a year and I could tell you cared more about yourself than him. It's no surprise you're turning to an invisible entity. Just like Mom. You thought she was bad our whole lives, after Dad passed she was borderline obsessive. That's the only reason I'm reading.
~~~

I want to know what the big deal is. Has he filed yet?"

"I…I don't know."

Her gaze softened. "I'm sorry this is happening again…"

I rolled my eyes and huffed out a breath. Part of me wanted to slap her. Mark and Sky were as silent as mice. I looked at Mark to make sure he hadn't passed out from the shock. His eyes flicked between us as he took in the information.

"Man, that's why you're all into God? Trying to fill the void? But I liked him," he said with his lip partially pouted, which caused a laugh to bubble out of my lips. It was a manic laugh of gratitude for a change of subject. I tried not to be offended. Of course, they wouldn't believe me. Rebekah didn't even understand our own mother's reasoning, let alone my own.

"You haven't been around for how many years? What do you mean you liked him? You hardly even knew him," I said while shaking my head, little chuckles flitting out.

"Yeah, but I know him like I know my nieces and nephews, which isn't very good. I still like them."

"You mean niece and nephew?"

"No, Bek's has kids too, you selfish hooligan," he said as he shrugged his shoulders.

I rolled my eyes. "Okay Mark, you got me there. What did you like that was better than the last four? Because you hated all of them."

CHAPTER SIXTEEN

Faith blooms

"Nevey? Earth to Nevey?"

I peered around. I was holding a breakfast sandwich I didn't even remember getting from the microwave. I looked down at it and back at Nate. "What happened?"

"You zoned out. I was telling you that you didn't need to worry, that I would take care of you and the kids as long as needed. You just shut down."

"Umm... Thanks."

"Care to tell me where you disappeared to for the last five minutes?"

Five minutes? Crap. I was already late for the service!

"I don't have time. We're already late." I sped away quickly and scooped Merkal up as I walked around the counter. When I looked back, I stopped. His face had fallen. He was focused on his coffee again and nodded to himself, as if agreeing to a conversation he was having.

"I'm sorry, that was rude."

His eyebrows rose, and he looked closer at me.

"I was thinking about a conversation I had with my brother, sister, and Sky. About how no one believes me about my faith. About how I'm not sure I even believe, but that I still have to go to figure it out."

He nodded his head and opened his mouth before he closed it. He tried again, but closed it. I tried to stay patient. Something inside told me he needed this moment. The service would still be there even if I was late.

"Are you really that committed?" he finally asked.

"I just, I've been reading my daddy's journals. There's this feeling I get Nate, this calm. I don't know how to explain it. It's not a numbness like when I drink… it's almost like it's bringing me back to life."

"I remember feeling like that. A long time ago," he said under his breath. "Can we talk when you get home?"

I nodded. He gave me a hesitant smile. My stomach filled with butterflies.

"Go on, you're late. Tell me how it is. What church are you going to?"

"It's called Grace," I whispered.

I held my breath as he stepped forward. He looked down at Merkal and then at me. He gave Merkal a kiss on the forehead, who giggled before he squirmed away. Time felt as if it stilled as he pulled back. He looked at me, his hand lifted and put a stray hair behind my ear. I sighed, the breath I had been holding burst out low and fast. He turned to Mysty, who had her arms crossed and was looking up at him with irritation. Nate chuckled and bent down to give her a kiss.

"You look beautiful," he said before he turned away. He walked to the coffee pot as I stared at him and filled his cup back up. "What? I was talking to Mysty," he said as he winked at me.

I shook my head to clear it and rolled my eyes.

"Go on," he said as he fluttered his hand to show us to leave.

~ ~ ~

The church was beautiful. It was a large building, painted with a crisp white. There was a pointed section that shot straight into the air with a cross placed heavily on the top of it. It was so big I could swear God himself had to put it up there.

I chuckled at the thought of a hand so large that it had to use its fingertips to pick it up.

"What are you laughing about?" Mysty said.

"Oh, nothing baby, what do you think?"

"It's pretty big. Do you think it's fake?"

"No baby, I have a feeling this is gonna be our church."

"Our very own church?" Merkal asked.

I laughed. We stood there holding hands for several seconds. I felt something bloom in my chest and work its way up through my head. "Yes, little bug, our very own church."

I felt Merkal tug on my hand as he began hopping in place. "Let's go. Let's go!" he shouted.

I shook my head and looked at Mysty. She seemed a little unsure. "You ready, princess?"

She looked at me, her eyes big as saucers. "Mama, I saw Grandma… she was waving for us to go inside."

I shot backwards and looked around. There wasn't anyone outside, but I could see someone standing inside looking out. He was waiting to open the door. Part of me wanted to run. Maybe this wasn't such a good idea.

"Maybe you saw the greeter, baby."

"No! It was Grandma. She was smiling, and she winked at me. Weird greeters don't wink at strangers. It was her. She was right there." She pointed just in front of the door. She was anxious to pull me forward. I felt like my feet had been glued to the cement parking lot.

"Mama, come on, Grandma told us to go here."

"Baby, Grandma's not here, remember? We talked about this. Grandma passed away. She's with God now. That's why we're learning about him.. so-"

She cut me off mid-sentence. "I know she's dead mama. How else would she be see through? How else would she fade away and drift into the sky?"

She had tears in her eyes as I looked down at her. I looked at Merkal, afraid she was scaring him.

"I saw her too, Mama. I heard her whisper."

"What'd she say baby?" I asked, desperate to know.

"Sacrifice. Faith. Love. Grow. Then she said God let her see us," he said as he shrugged his shoulders. He chewed on his lip. "What does that mean?"

"I think I know. Come on."

They put on brave faces. I tried to follow their example; they were more excited than I was to move forward. I kept going, despite my doubt.

Let it go, a soft voice whispered in my head. When we got to the door, what felt like a millennium later, the greeter opened it. I forced a smile.

"Welcome, welcome! To Grace, where even the most lost can be found and saved."

My eyes widened. Found by grace. Saved by grace. What an interesting concept.

"And who are these beautiful little ones?"

"Oh, uh, this is Mysty, and Merkal."

"I'm six," Mysty said proudly. She puffed out her chest and stood on her toes.

"Wow," the man said. "How old are you, Merkal?"

Merkal studied him for a second. He held up his toddler hand with four fingers sticking up.

"Man. We have some little adults here in service today." He turned to me. "Would you like them to be in service with you- uh… I didn't catch your name?"

"Oh.." I laughed. "My name is Nevaeh. But everyone calls me Nevey."

"Wow, what a beautiful name. I'll bet a name with that kind of power hasn't made life easy."

"You have no idea."

He smiled warmly. "Well, I want to say a very heartfelt welcome. Let everything you have been through go and enjoy the service. I'll show you the children's section. Is Merkal in kindergarten yet?"

"Actually yes, he's starting in a week with his sister, her birthday fell in a weird spot so this is her first year in Kinder."

"They make it fun with the way the dates fall, don't they?"

I nodded my head in agreement and began to run a hand through my hair, but I forgot I'd put it in a braid. I dropped my hand awkwardly.

"Shall we?" he said, while still beaming.

I nodded and followed him. "Up, up, up," Merkal said nervously. I stooped down and picked him up, while also still moving forward.

"Mama, I want up to," Mysty said.

I sighed, but relented and put one on each hip.

"Wow, you have your hands full with those two."

I smiled sweetly. "Eh, it's not all bad. I get like ten workouts a day."

He chuckled as we came to a low set counter. It had a small door pinned against it and the wall. Beyond that was the enormous expanse of a room about the size of a classroom. It looked like Mysty's preschool classroom, but with fewer toys.

"Down, down, down!" both Mysty and Merkal chanted.

"Shh, not so loud." I chastised.

They squirmed out of my arms, and I rolled my eyes.

"They're alright, we love kids here. If you sign in here, once you've come for a couple more times and if you want to become a part of the church we will put you in the system."

I nodded, as if I knew what that meant. I didn't enjoy feeling dumb. How ironic, when I was here to figure out if I really believed in God.

He opened the gate and both of them took off before I could even kiss them. "Well, see you later then," I said, only partially offended.

Home. It felt like home. I watched them for several more seconds as their giggles filled the room and they ran up to a few other children.

Amazing. How children easily approached people with genuine care and openness. Without regret or fear of being rejected. Without being offended, even if they were.

"Would you like me to show you where the service takes place?"

I jumped. He was standing next to me, and I'd forgotten. I watched a woman as she guided the kids to a table so they could color a paper.

"I'm sorry. I didn't mean to scare you," he said quickly.

"Oh, uh, no you're fine. I just love seeing how happy they are."

"Oh yeah, all the kids love being here. They do group sessions just like in school. But, there's time for that later. Can I show you where the service takes place? We call it the sanctuary."

"Of course. What was your name?"

"Oh! I'm sorry, it's Justin. I've been here at Grace for fifteen years. I'm sure you will love it."

"I already do."

He smiled broadly at me, and we walked the opposite way we'd come.

"I'm sure they're still doing worship. Hopefully you like to sing because everyone loves singing here."

"I don't think anyone wants to hear my voice. I couldn't place a tune if you spelled it out for me."

He chuckled and shook his head. "If God doesn't judge the wanderer, why would he judge a person for having a terrible voice? He just wants us to value him and show we love him like he does us."

I'd never thought of singing off key as showing that you valued a person. "I have a question."

"Sure! What can I help with?"

"Well, to be frank, I'm still trying to figure out if I believe or not. This is the fifth church I've been to."

"My dear, if you've been to five churches, I'm pretty sure you believe." He looked sidelong at me and grinned knowingly. "You may wander, but you will always be found and guided back to his side."

"But why? Why do you believe, and why do you think I already believe?"

He put his hand on his chest. "You feel that?"

"Umm.. sorry what? I'm not the one with my hand on my chest. Are you talking about your heartbeat?"

He chuckled. The sound made his entire body shake. "Oh dear, you really are lost." He pursed his lips, but it wasn't in irritation, it was in a calm understanding. "I don't know what your life looks like, but that feeling? Even if you don't recognize it now, that feeling of emptiness that seems to dissipate, and somehow feels filled sometimes? That, my dear, is God. That, my dear, is true love."

I tilted my head to the side. Two months ago, I would have told him to eat rocks and flipped him the bird, but with everything I'd felt, and not felt over the last month, some part of me knew he was right.

"Alright! Here we are. Maybe some of your doubts and questions will be answered today."

"Thank you for being so welcoming."

"If I wasn't welcoming, well, I would hope you would pray for me," he said as he winked and walked away.

I shook my head. What an odd man.

CHAPTER SEVENTEEN

Loved

I felt awkward, maybe because I was late. Maybe because every church I had gone to over the last five weeks had made me feel uncomfortable and I didn't have the distraction of my babies this time. Everyone smiled and nodded at me. Several faces that blended together welcomed me as I walked down the aisles to a sit away from everyone. I wanted to see what this God everyone was talking about had to say today.

As the worship came to an end and I swayed to the sound of the music, what I assumed was the Pastor walked on the stage and began speaking. "Wow… God is in the house this morning. I couldn't have said it better myself. God is speaking to us to take action. To open ourselves, to be fueled and nourished by his love."

He looked around the room before continuing, "I had a sermon today. I'd planned something regarding the holiday coming up, but as I was going over my notes last night, something changed. We just ended our lessons in the book of Nehemiah, and usually I would continue on into Esther, but we are jumping to John. John 1-41 to be exact. Welcome everyone. If you are new, we are so glad to have you here. I am pastor Randall, and this house is your house."

He walked across the stage and stepped down. He shook hands with several people before he walked back on stage.

"A woman, who Jesus had no business talking to. A woman without a name, but one that Jesus asked to bring him water. Let us read through it."

My chest constricted. A breath pushed through my lips. Oh no, why am I gonna cry now? Everyone's gonna think I'm nuts. I looked at my phone to dim the overwhelming feeling crashing through my body. It was slicing through and out of control. I left nothing on my phone to distract me. Nate had messaged me to say he hoped I enjoyed the service, but it only made my heart clinch further.

"The woman at the well. What a beautiful story. A woman who had every reason to doubt the messiah but ached and craved to be filled with the water only he could provide. A sacrificial love. A love he openly gave in trust, despite her mistakes and weakness. Jesus knew he could use her!"

The pastor pushed his bible up toward the ceiling. He paced back and forth as he continued speaking. "Jesus displayed love toward a woman he had no reason to. A woman he knew he could trust to share his word, even with her faults. God trusts us to spread his word. Why does God allow so much pain, you might ask? My own mother died from a brain aneurism. Why? She loved God! Why didn't he just start over? If his creation was so brutally driven, then why not start over?"

I nodded my head in agreement. Why indeed? To watch his so-called children, suffer? I would never do that for my own children. I hunched forward under the weight of all I was feeling. The confusion, loss, betrayal, anger, resentment, and broken heartedness.

"Love! That's what! We weren't a mistake. God is incapable of making mistakes. Only we are. Only we are sinners. But yet… because he is love.. the love. He loves us, anyway. He trusts us, despite our faults to spread his word. To spread the gift, he gives us. Only God can fill the void in your heart. That void of entanglement because of your own selfishness and sins. Jesus died for you, so that you may live! Now it's you who has to step out in faith. It's you who has to except that life bringing love."

He jabbed his finger toward the crowd. An accusatory finger that left the weight crushing me. I cried, and I wasn't even sure why.

"It's you who has to step toward him. He is waiting for you to take his hand! For you to trust him and trust the faith you can feel brimming under the surface."

I shuddered, feeling as if he was talking to me. He held out his hand, as if to grab all of ours and pull us along with him on stage.

"God is with us this morning, asking in whispers and waiting for you to hold out your hand to him. Will you obey? If you feel a burden needing to be lifted, if you are drowning in the struggles of your life, leave your shame at the door. Come forward and lay your burdens at his feet. Cast your fear and doubt aside! Come forward, as the woman at the well did. Before she knew he was the messiah, she begged for his living water. She had faith that he would be honest and lift her, filling her void. He can do that for you as well!"

I didn't realize I was moving until I was already standing in front of the cross. I didn't know what to do, but my knees buckled and I collapsed to the floor. I crossed my hands and sobbed. I was talking before I even knew what to say.

"I let go God! I believe in you. Please, Father, take me as I am, every flawed part. Take my marriage, my loss, my pain, my mistakes and lift them from my shoulders! Take me, father, forgive me, fill me with your love. I want to know you! To know this! To know your love!"

I cried out and sobbed at that cross, slumped against the lip of it, placed against the floor of the stage for several minutes. I stayed in place and fell apart, my head bent forward as he finished the sermon. My body felt as if someone had fractured it and lay it in small broken pieces at the foot of that cross. I cried out; my heart split open. I felt raw, but as I fell apart, something inside was stitching me back together. The heartbreak didn't feel so broken anymore. The pain not so unbearable. The tears no longer tears of pain, but tears of realization and acceptance, of submission.

"I trust you God. I want to know you. Take me, Father, and lift me up."

I didn't realize several of the congregation had noticed my fall. I was surrounded by people with their hands on me as they prayed. They repeated what they heard come from my lips, or what was on their own hearts. Home. This felt right. This felt like home. I felt like I was being filled, and I never wanted to go back to being empty again.

EPILOGUE

"Saved By Grace"

When I got home from service that day, it was as if Nate recognized something had changed. We sat down while the kiddos took a nap and discussed things. How he didn't really want a divorce, but he felt trapped, unsure how he could do more to be a better husband. I felt the same way about being a wife. We'd failed each other miserably. Not realizing we didn't know how to love properly. We agreed to work with each other. We agreed to try.

He admitted he was weary and tired of the difficulties. I admitted I was empty, but God was filling me with something I didn't need to look for outside gratification from.

I continuously repeat to myself the words he finished the conversation with when I felt doubt or confusion; "I heard somewhere once, sometimes God has to let you be emptied in order to fill you back up."

It took almost three months, but as I continued, our children became more excited and transfixed in learning about God. Nate suddenly asked to join me for service one Sunday. I met the lord at the cross that day, not in repent, but in gratitude. My heart now felt full, and God was teaching us both how to love properly.

As the months went by, I felt a tug on my heart to forgive those who had done me wrong, or that I felt had. Forgiving wasn't enough, though. God put it on my heart to reach out to them. It wasn't easy, and to be honest, for a while I refused. Eventually, as the tug pulled harder and wouldn't go away, I reached out to my brother and apologized for everything. I understood his pain, his emptiness, and I forgave him for lashing out. He never responded, but God made sure to let me know he was proud of my efforts.

I still poured over my daddy's journals. I was always learning new things, and it seemed like when I had a question, I could find it in those pages. I was always discovering new answers to questions I had. There didn't seem to be just one answer. Daddy had asked God how to let go of something we couldn't control, to let go of people who we can't seem to get to forgive us. God's answer was simple. To love, to pray, to let go. Daddy also asked questions about knowing people's intentions. That he could feel when someone had ill will toward him. God's answer was simple. That we couldn't read others' minds and hearts, only he could. I tried to follow that advice closely. It was hard.

The months coursed by, unapologetic, and things began to change. God blessed us. Nate and I had a set of twins exactly a year to the date that Nate had told me he wanted a divorce.

Sky and Rebekah saw my change firsthand. They sat idly by and watched wearily. They admitted they expected me to turn my cheek when Nate and I worked things out and our son fought for his life with a brain tumor. Through prayer and dedication, Merkal survived and healed.

Rebekah, Sky, and I began to have weekly study sessions. We called it Chai addicts and God talk. We posted videos together, going through the books of the bible with strong female women. Women led to God by their faith and trauma. We talked about our own revelation and interviewed women who had trauma they overcame with the strength of God at their center.

Mark found a woman one day when he decided to go to a service with me, finally convinced my change wasn't a scam. Lorelli had gone to the church for five years and was part of the children's ministry. They got married six months later. They are still married five years later and have two beautiful children.

Life isn't easy. If anything, it's gotten harder.

Some days I struggle, but on those days I approach it with grace and kindness to myself and those around me, or at least try to. I pray hard on those days. To be led, despite the mountains I have to climb and the enemy waiting in the shadow. To be filled everyday by our Fathers love, allowing it to spill onto those I encounter.

For that, I can only be eternally grateful I was saved by His grace.

"It only takes one act of faith to spark a revolution of change. A revolution to LOVE as God loves us."

-Brittany K Moore

THE END.

Made in the USA
Monee, IL
25 July 2023

39863656R00100